HER KINGDOM, HER CREATION

A JOURNEY OF AMBITION AND EMPOWERMENT

SANDHIYA IYYAPPAN

To every woman who dares to dream bigger than the limitations placed upon her, to those who rise from humble beginnings to forge their own paths, and to the unwavering spirit of resilience that dwells within each of us. This story is dedicated to you – the architects of your own destinies, the builders of empires, the champions of your dreams. It's a testament to the incredible power of believing in yourselves, even when the odds seem insurmountable. May this tale inspire you to chase your ambitions relentlessly, embrace your unique strengths, and never, ever underestimate the magnitude of your potential. Your journey is not just your own; it's a source of inspiration for generations to come. May this book serve as a beacon, illuminating the path toward your own extraordinary achievements. Your strength, your courage, your determination – these are the cornerstones of a brighter future, not just for you, but for the world. Embrace your power. You are capable of anything you set your mind to.

Contents

Contents

Preface

Samantha's story resonated deeply with me, perhaps because it mirrors so many of the experiences I've witnessed in my own life and through the journeys of other remarkable women I've had the privilege of knowing. As a female entrepreneur and writer, I've navigated my share of challenges and triumphs – the exhilarating highs and the soul-crushing lows that come with building a business from the ground up. In Samantha, I saw a reflection of that struggle, a raw and honest portrayal of the grit, determination, and unwavering belief in oneself required to succeed against all odds. Her journey is not a fairy tale, but a powerful testament to the resilience of the human spirit and the transformative power of embracing one's ambitions. This story isn't just about the building of a business empire; it's about the building of a woman – the forging of a strong, independent identity, the cultivation of unwavering selfbelief, and the unwavering loyalty to those who stand by you on the journey. I hope that as you read Samantha's story, you'll find inspiration not just in her success, but in the unwavering spirit that propelled her to achieve it. I hope it ignites a spark within you to pursue your own dreams, no matter how audacious they may seem.

Acknowledgements

First and foremost, I want to express my deepest gratitude to the countless women who have inspired this story. Your resilience, determination, and unwavering spirit in the face of adversity are a testament to the power of the human spirit. This book is dedicated to all women. Thank you for making my writing experience feels so powerful, both implicitly and explicitly, and for showing the world what it means to be truly powerful.

My heartfelt appreciation extends to my family, whose patience and understanding made this journey possible. Your love and support have been my constant source of strength.

Introduction

The Australian outback, vast and unforgiving yet breathtakingly beautiful, serves as the backdrop to Samantha's extraordinary journey. From the humble beginnings in a small, isolated town, Samantha's entrepreneurial spirit ignited, fueled by a yearning for something more, a drive to create a life far beyond the confines of her familiar surroundings. This is a story of a woman who dared to challenge expectations, who refused to be defined by her circumstances. It's a story of audacious dreams, unwavering determination, and the unwavering strength to overcome seemingly insurmountable obstacles. Follow Samantha as she navigates the treacherous terrain of the business world, from initial setbacks and funding rejections to building a formidable empire. Witness her resilience in the face of adversity, her unwavering loyalty to those she trusts, and her steadfast commitment to her values. This isn't a story solely about financial success, but about personal growth, about the evolution of a woman who dares to define her own path. Samantha's journey is a powerful reminder that the most significant achievements are not merely about accumulating wealth, but about forging your own identity, staying true to your values, and leaving an indelible mark on the world. Prepare to be inspired by a woman who embodies the true spirit of female empowerment and entrepreneurial success. Prepare to be inspired by the Outback Empress.

CHAPTER 1
Samantha's Humble Beginnings

———◦♡◦———

The sun beat down on Samantha's shoulders, a relentless Australian sun that baked the red earth until it shimmered with heat. She was twelve, small for her age, but her movements were purposeful as she wrestled a stubborn bale of hay, her muscles straining with the effort. The air hung heavy with the scent of dust and eucalyptus, a fragrance she would carry with her always, a reminder of her humble beginnings in the heart of the outback. Her family's farm, a sprawling expanse of dusty plains and sparse vegetation, was both her prison and her playground. It was a life of hard work, of sunrises before dawn and sunsets after dusk, a life where resilience was not a virtue but a necessity. She knew the rhythm of the land, the unpredictable moods of the weather, the tireless demands of farming life. It was a life that instilled in her a deep respect for nature and an unshakeable work ethic.

Her home, a simple weatherboard house with a corrugated iron roof, sat perched on a slight rise overlooking the parched landscape. It was modest, even by outback standards, but it was filled with the warmth of family. Her parents, hardworking and stoic, instilled in her a strong sense of values – honesty, integrity, and a fierce independence. They taught her not just how to work the land, but how to find strength in the face of adversity, a lesson the harsh outback environment readily provided. Evenings were often spent around a crackling fire, the flickering flames illuminating faces etched with the wisdom of years spent battling the elements. Stories of their own struggles, their perseverance, their triumphs over drought and hardship – these were the lessons that shaped young Samantha.

Samantha wasn't just a passive participant in farm life. Even at a young age, she displayed a remarkable entrepreneurial spirit, a spark of ingenuity that burned bright beneath the surface. She started small, tending to a small patch of land she'd claimed as her own, experimenting with different crops, learning which ones thrived in the harsh climate and which ones withered and died. She'd trade her surplus produce with neighbors, bartering for things she couldn't grow herself – eggs from Mrs. Gable, homemade jams from old Mr. Fitzwilliam. These small transactions were her first lessons in business, her early experiments in supply and demand. She learned the value of hard work, the importance of resourcefulness, and the satisfaction of a successful trade, all within the confines of her small, isolated world.

Her world was small, but her dreams were vast. She'd gaze at the endless expanse of the starry sky, a sky so full of stars it seemed to spill over onto the earth, and dream of a life beyond the farm, a life that held the promise of adventure and challenges that the outback couldn't offer. She devoured books, borrowing any she could find from the dusty shelves of the small town library. The stories within transported her to faraway lands, introducing her to different cultures, different lives, and different possibilities. She dreamt of cities shimmering with lights, of bustling streets and towering buildings, a stark contrast to the quiet stillness of her rural existence. These dreams weren't mere fantasies; they fueled her ambition, a relentless fire that burned within her, whispering promises of a future far removed from the familiar landscape of her youth.

The limitations of her small town were palpable. Opportunities were scarce, and the future seemed predetermined. For most girls her age, the path was clear: marriage, family, and a life tied to the land. But Samantha refused to accept such limitations. She yearned for more, for a life that stretched beyond the horizons of her small town, a life where she could shape her own destiny, a life that was hers alone to build. This deep-seated desire for something more, this unwavering belief in her own potential, would become her driving force. It would push her to overcome obstacles, to defy expectations, and ultimately, to build a business empire from the ground up.

Her days were filled with the mundane tasks of farm life, but her mind was often elsewhere, a million thoughts swirling through her head, ideas sparked by the everyday challenges of life in the outback. She observed, she analyzed, she searched for solutions to problems that others seemed to accept as inevitable. She saw inefficiency in the way things were done, opportunities overlooked, needs unmet. These observations were more than just passing thoughts. They were the seeds of her future enterprise, the inspiration that would one day blossom into a successful business. She learned to see possibilities where others saw limitations, a talent that would serve her well in the years to come.

Her evenings were spent learning, growing, and planning. She devoured books on business, finance, and marketing, educating herself through sheer determination and unwavering persistence. She'd spend hours poring over industry reports, analyzing market trends, and sketching out rudimentary business plans on scraps of paper. She used every available resource, attending local workshops and connecting with anyone who possessed even a shred of business knowledge. She was a sponge, soaking up information and applying it to the development of her own ideas. Her thirst for knowledge, her unwavering dedication to self-improvement, were a testament to her relentless ambition and her unyielding belief in her own potential.

The stark beauty of the outback, often unforgiving, provided a crucible in which her resilience was forged. The isolation, though initially confining, became a breeding ground for creativity and self-reliance. She learned to rely on her own instincts, to trust her own judgement, to make decisions without the crutch of readily available advice. The solitude allowed her to focus, to hone her skills, and to cultivate the inner strength that would be essential to her future success. The challenges she faced in the outback weren't merely obstacles; they were stepping stones, each one bringing her closer to the realization of her dreams.

The contrast between the vast, unforgiving landscape and her burgeoning ambition was striking. The endless expanse of the outback represented the seemingly limitless possibilities before her, while the confines of her small-town life highlighted the challenges she would have to overcome to reach her goals. This constant interplay between limitation and possibility fueled her drive, giving her the strength to push forward even when the path ahead seemed insurmountable. It was this tension, this duality, that would shape her character and define her journey from a girl with a dream in the Australian outback to a powerful businesswoman illuminating the city lights. Her story was only just beginning.

CHAPTER 2
The Spark of an Idea

The relentless sun dipped below the horizon, painting the sky in fiery hues of orange and purple. Samantha, her face streaked with dust and sweat, leaned against a weathered fence post, the rhythmic creak a familiar lullaby. The day's work was done, but her mind was far from still. The image of Mrs. Gable, the elderly woman who lived at the edge of the property, struggling to carry her weekly shopping, replayed in her mind. Mrs. Gable's small frame, bent under the weight of groceries, was a stark contrast to the vast expanse of the outback. It was a picture of vulnerability, a silent scream against the indifference of the landscape.

That night, under a sky dusted with a million stars, the seed of an idea took root. Samantha had always been resourceful, a necessity born from her upbringing. She'd learned to fix broken fences, mend clothes, and even build makeshift toys from scraps of wood and wire. But this was different. This wasn't about patching a hole in a fence or repairing a broken toy; this was about solving a problem, about offering a tangible solution to a real need in her community. The idea was simple, almost embarrassingly so: a delivery service for the isolated farms and homesteads scattered across the outback.

The simplicity, however, belied the enormity of the challenge. Samantha had no car, no phone, no money – nothing but an idea and a fierce determination. The doubts gnawed at her. What if it didn't work? What if she was foolish to even attempt such a thing? Her family, though supportive in their quiet, hardworking way, hadn't the means to provide financial backing. The vast distances, the unpredictable weather, the sheer logistics of it all felt overwhelming. The initial enthusiasm started to wane, replaced by a wave of self-doubt.

She spent sleepless nights wrestling with the practicality of her plan. How would she transport the goods? A bicycle was too slow and unreliable; a motorbike was beyond her financial reach. Then there was the problem of communication. How would she receive orders and coordinate deliveries without a phone? Her initial excitement morphed into frustration, the raw, untamed energy of her initial inspiration slowly being stifled by a sense of impossibility.

The reality of the situation crashed down upon her with the force of a sudden dust storm. She'd envisioned herself zooming around on a motorbike, a modern-day outback mail carrier, delivering goods with efficiency and grace. The reality was far more mundane, and considerably more daunting. She was a twelve-year-old girl with nothing but a dream and a well-worn bicycle. The chasm between the vision and the reality was vast, and for a moment, she felt paralysed by it.

But the image of Mrs. Gable, her frail frame bent under the weight of groceries, remained stubbornly imprinted on Samantha's mind. The memory of the old woman's grateful smile when Samantha had once helped her carry her shopping bag acted as an anchor, pulling her back from the brink of despair. That small act of kindness had sown the seed of empathy, and that empathy was now fueling her resolve.

Samantha's initial brainstorming sessions were less sophisticated strategy meetings and more chaotic scribbles in the margins of her schoolbooks. She drew maps of the local area, painstakingly marking the location of every house and homestead. She calculated distances, estimated travel times, and considered various methods of transport, each one fraught with challenges. She dreamt of a fleet of vehicles, a team of helpers, a thriving business. But the reality was a battered bicycle, a few empty grocery bags, and a whole lot of grit.

She started small, focusing on Mrs. Gable and a few other elderly residents in her immediate vicinity. She used her bicycle, relying on word of mouth to spread the news of her service. The early days were fraught with difficulties. The summer heat was relentless, the terrain rough, and the distances daunting. Many times, she felt like giving up, the weight of her ambition crushing her spirit. The lack of resources, the feeling of isolation, and the constant nagging voice of self-doubt were her constant companions.

However, with each successful delivery, a small ember of hope began to glow. The gratitude in the eyes of her clients, the feeling of accomplishment with each completed task, and the satisfaction of knowing she had made a difference, slowly began to outweigh the challenges. The small act of kindness, that had started as a simple gesture of helping a neighbour, had evolved into something far greater - it had become the genesis of her entrepreneurial journey.

The initial struggle was not just about logistics or resources; it was a battle fought within herself. It was a struggle against her own self-doubt, a wrestling match with the fear of failure. She wrestled with questions of feasibility, capability, and the possibility of success in a world seemingly designed to keep her down. The outback had taught her resilience, but the city lights, with their relentless competition and overwhelming scale, represented a different kind of challenge. This was a fight she was facing alone, armed only with her determination and her belief in her idea.

The lessons were harsh but invaluable. She learned the hard way that planning, while important, wasn't everything. Flexibility, adaptability, and a willingness to adjust her approach based on unforeseen circumstances were crucial to her survival. She learned that setbacks were inevitable, but that they should be viewed not as failures, but as opportunities to learn and grow.

Slowly but surely, Samantha began refining her initial idea, transforming it into a more structured and sustainable business model. The challenges were plentiful; every step forward was met with setbacks. The process of converting a raw idea into a viable business plan was a torturous one, a constant process of trial and error, modification and adaptation. But the determination, fueled by her resilience and empathy, helped her navigate the complexities of the entrepreneurial world.

Her experiences taught her valuable lessons about resource management, marketing, customer service, and the importance of building strong relationships. She learned that success wasn't a destination, but a continuous process of learning, adapting, and refining. Her journey from a girl with a dream in the outback to a budding entrepreneur in her small town was far from smooth, but it was a journey of constant growth and self-discovery. The spark of an idea, ignited by a simple act of kindness, had set her on a path that would lead her far beyond the dusty plains and into the dazzling lights of the city. The journey had just begun, but she was ready, armed with grit, determination, and the unwavering belief in her ability to succeed. The outback had given her resilience, and the need of her community had given her purpose. Now, she was ready to build something remarkable.

CHAPTER 3
Facing Initial Hurdles

The chipped paint on the desk of the loan officer seemed to mock Samantha's meticulously crafted business plan. She'd spent weeks, months even, pouring over spreadsheets, crafting projections that felt more like hopeful prayers than solid financial forecasts. Now, sitting across from Mr. Henderson, a man whose expression could curdle milk, she felt the familiar knot of anxiety tighten in her stomach. He'd barely glanced at her presentation, his eyes flitting between her and the clock on the wall, a silent countdown to her inevitable dismissal.

"Ms. Jones," he'd finally said, his voice devoid of warmth, "while your passion is admirable, the risk is simply too high. A start-up in the sustainable cosmetics industry… it's a niche market. We can't justify the loan."

The rejection felt like a physical blow, a punch to the gut that stole the air from her lungs. She'd anticipated this, of course. She'd braced herself for the inevitable "no's," but hearing it aloud, seeing the dismissive glint in his eyes, still stung. The carefully constructed optimism she'd maintained throughout the preparation crumbled slightly at the edges.

Leaving the bank, Samantha felt the weight of the city pressing down on her. The bustling crowds, the honking cars, the relentless energy that had once exhilarated her now felt suffocating. The vibrant city lights, symbols of opportunity just weeks ago, now seemed to mock her ambition. She walked, her head bowed, replaying the meeting in her mind, searching for a flaw in her presentation, a missed opportunity to convince Mr. Henderson. But there was nothing. Her plan was sound, her passion undeniable. It was simply a matter of convincing someone to take a chance.

That night, curled up on her tiny apartment couch, the city lights casting long shadows across the room, Samantha allowed herself to feel the crushing weight of despair. Doubt, a unwelcome guest, crept into her thoughts. Had she been foolish to leave the familiar comfort of her outback life? Was this audacious dream, this vision of a sustainable beauty empire, nothing more than a pipe dream? Tears welled in her eyes, unshed, held back by a stubborn refusal to surrender.

But the tears weren't just tears of defeat. They were tears of frustration, of exhaustion, of the sheer relentless pressure of chasing a dream against the odds. They were also, however, tears fueled by an unyielding inner fire. She'd spent years building this dream, nurtured it through sleepless nights and countless hours of hard work. She had faced setbacks before – the harsh realities of outback life had taught her resilience. This was just another hurdle, a particularly steep one, but not insurmountable.

The next morning, she woke with a renewed sense of purpose. The despair had subsided, replaced by a quiet determination. She wouldn't let this one rejection define her. She'd approach other investors, refine her pitch, and seek out alternative funding sources. She began researching angel investors, scouring online forums and attending networking events, even reaching out to women entrepreneurs she admired, hoping for mentorship and guidance. Each "no" she received was a lesson, a refinement of her strategy, a step closer to a "yes."

She learned to pitch her story with more precision, highlighting the market need for sustainable cosmetics, emphasizing the potential for growth, and focusing on the unique selling points of her products. She discovered that the key wasn't just having a solid business plan, but also telling a compelling story, a story that resonated with the investor's values and aspirations.

She received countless rejections, emails that landed unread in her inbox, phone calls that never came. There were days when the weight of it all felt unbearable. The loneliness of the entrepreneurial journey pressed down on her, a heavy cloak that threatened to smother her spirit. But she found solace in small victories, a positive comment here, a supportive message there, each a tiny spark that kept her flame alive.

She stumbled upon a women's entrepreneurial support group, a haven where she found camaraderie and encouragement. Sharing her struggles with other women facing similar challenges fostered a sense of community, a reminder that she wasn't alone in this fight. They shared tips, resources, and most importantly, unwavering support, bolstering her confidence and reminding her of the power of collective strength.

One particularly challenging day, after a particularly scathing rejection from a venture capitalist, she found herself sitting at a small café, nursing a lukewarm coffee, feeling utterly defeated. A woman at the next table, noticing her distress, approached her. Her name was Clara, and she'd built a successful organic food business from the ground up. They talked for hours, Clara sharing her own story of setbacks, perseverance, and eventual triumph.

Clara's story was a testament to the resilience of the human spirit, a beacon of hope in Samantha's otherwise bleak landscape. She shared invaluable insights, strategies that had helped her secure funding, and ways to navigate the complex world of venture capital. More than that, Clara instilled in Samantha a newfound belief in herself, a reaffirmation of her ability to overcome these challenges.

The turning point came unexpectedly, through a serendipitous encounter at a sustainability conference. Samantha had attended, hoping to network and learn from industry leaders. She presented her business plan to a panel of judges, her voice steady, her confidence bolstered by the support she'd received from Clara and the women's group. Her passion shone through, her vision resonated with the audience, and she was awarded a small grant, enough to get her business off the ground.

This wasn't the huge investment she'd initially sought, but it was enough. It was a lifeline, a validation of her vision, and a testament to her unwavering determination. The grant provided her with the seed capital she needed to finally start producing her sustainable cosmetics line, to rent a small workshop, and to begin building her brand.

The journey had been arduous, a relentless uphill climb filled with setbacks and disappointments. But Samantha had learned invaluable lessons along the way. She'd learned about resilience, about the power of community, about the importance of believing in herself, even when everyone else doubted her. She'd discovered the strength that lay within, the fierce determination that would not let her surrender her dreams. The city lights, once symbols of her frustration, now represented the limitless possibilities that lay ahead, illuminated by the unwavering light of her own ambition. The outback had prepared her for this, shaped her character, forged her resilience. Now, she was ready to conquer the city, one sustainable lipstick at a time.

CHAPTER 4

First Steps Towards Success

The air in the small, rented studio apartment crackled with a nervous energy that belied the quiet hum of the industrial sewing machine. Samantha, her fingers stained with vibrant pigments and her face flushed with exertion, carefully applied a final layer of shimmering, organic lipstick to a sample tube. This wasn't just any lipstick; this was *Earth Hues* , her brainchild, her dream poured into a sleek, sustainable tube. The loan had been denied, of course, but that hadn't stopped her. She'd mortgaged her tiny outback cottage, her grandmother's legacy, a decision that still sent a shiver down her spine, but one she knew was necessary. This was her chance.

The first few sales were tentative, a trickle rather than a flood. She'd set up a small online store, relying on word-ofmouth and the power of social media, a platform she'd reluctantly learned to navigate. Each order, each positive review, felt like a small victory, a validation of the countless hours she'd poured into perfecting her formula, her packaging, her brand. The feedback was invaluable. Women raved about the natural ingredients, the vibrant colors, the feeling of supporting a small, ethical business. She listened to their comments, noting what resonated and what needed tweaking. A deeper plum shade, a more matte finish, a more sustainable packaging option – each suggestion fueled her passion and shaped her product development.

Managing her resources was a constant tightrope walk. Every dollar was accounted for, every purchase meticulously planned.

She bartered services with local artists for website design and social media marketing, trading her expertise in natural cosmetics for their digital skills. This collaborative approach, born out of necessity, became a core value of her business. She realized that building a community wasn't just a marketing strategy; it was the lifeblood of her enterprise.

The initial growth was organic, fueled by passion and word of mouth. But as demand increased, Samantha faced a new set of challenges. She found herself overwhelmed, juggling order fulfillment, marketing, product development, and customer service – all single-handedly. The loneliness was palpable, a stark contrast to the vibrant community she'd built online. She realized she couldn't do it all alone.

This realization, though daunting, led her to one of her most significant decisions: building a team. She hesitated at first. The idea of relinquishing control, of entrusting her vision to others, felt terrifying. But she recognized that her own limitations were hindering her growth. Her first hire was Sarah, a young graphic designer with a passion for sustainable businesses and a talent for creating visually stunning marketing materials. Sarah brought not only technical skills, but also fresh ideas and boundless energy, breathing new life into the brand.

Then came Emily, a seasoned logistics expert who streamlined the fulfillment process, reducing shipping times and minimizing waste. Emily's efficiency allowed Samantha to focus on product development and marketing, areas where her creativity and passion truly shone. With each new team member, Samantha's vision expanded, evolving beyond her initial constraints. She learned the delicate balance of delegating tasks while maintaining her creative direction, trusting her team to execute her vision with their own unique expertise. She learned the art of collaborative leadership, recognizing the value of diverse perspectives and celebrating the individual strengths of her team.

Unexpected hurdles still arose. A batch of lipstick experienced a color inconsistency, requiring a costly recall and a painful lesson in quality control. A competitor launched a similar product, forcing Samantha to re-evaluate her marketing strategy and sharpen her competitive edge. Each setback, though initially discouraging, served as a learning opportunity. She learned to adapt, to pivot, to remain agile in the face of adversity. She learned that resilience wasn't the absence of setbacks, but the ability to bounce back stronger, wiser, and more determined.

The growth wasn't linear; it was a rollercoaster ride of highs and lows. There were days when she felt utterly overwhelmed, questioning her choices, doubting her abilities. But those were the days she leaned on her team, her community, her unwavering belief in her vision. She reminded herself of the outback, of the resilience it had instilled in her, of the unwavering belief in herself that had carried her through countless challenges.

The financial burden was considerable. The initial investment, coupled with the ongoing expenses of running a business, put a considerable strain on her resources. She had to make tough choices, prioritizing expenses and streamlining processes to maintain profitability. She learned about budgeting, cash flow management, and the importance of financial planning, skills that were far removed from her initial artistic aspirations but were essential to the success of her enterprise. She also learned to negotiate better deals with suppliers, leveraging her growing influence in the market to secure more favorable terms.

Slowly, steadily, Earth Hues blossomed. Her small, online store grew into a thriving e-commerce platform, receiving orders from across the country. She secured distribution deals with several boutique retailers, further expanding her reach and brand visibility. The small, rented studio apartment was replaced by a larger office space, a testament to her hard work and dedication.

Samantha's success wasn't just about financial gain; it was about creating a business that aligned with her values. Her commitment to sustainability, ethical sourcing, and fair labor practices resonated with her customers, fostering a loyal and passionate community. This community wasn't just a collection of consumers; it was a network of supporters, advocates, and fellow believers in her mission. They celebrated her successes and offered support during the inevitable setbacks.

The city lights, once a symbol of her daunting ambition, now reflected the warmth of her accomplishments. They represented not only the success of her business but also the strength of her character, the unwavering determination that had carried her from the outback to the city, from a lone entrepreneur to the leader of a growing team, from a dream to a thriving reality. The journey had been arduous, filled with challenges and sacrifices, but the rewards were far greater than she had ever imagined. And it was just the beginning. The foundation was laid, the future was bright, and Samantha, armed with her resilience, her team, and her unwavering belief in herself, was ready to face whatever came next. The outback had taught her grit; the city was teaching her the art of scaling her success. The future, with its dazzling city lights, shimmered with the promise of even greater achievements, painted in the vibrant hues of her own making.

CHAPTER 5
Building a Strong Foundation

The scent of drying herbs and beeswax still clung to her clothes, a comforting reminder of the long hours spent perfecting her all-natural lipstick formulas. The initial rush of launching *Earth Hues* had subsided, replaced by the quiet, focused determination that characterized Samantha's approach to building something truly lasting. The city lights, once a symbol of her audacious ambition, now served as a backdrop to her meticulous planning. She understood that the initial burst of success wasn't enough; she needed to build a foundation sturdy enough to weather any storm.

Her first priority was her customers. She wasn't just selling lipstick; she was building relationships. Every order was carefully packaged, accompanied by a handwritten note thanking the customer and offering personalized advice on using the product. She responded to every email, every social media message, fostering a community around her brand. She remembered the isolation of the outback, the feeling of being disconnected, and she vowed to make her customers feel seen and heard. This wasn't just good customer service; it was a strategic move to cultivate brand loyalty. She organized online Q&A sessions, inviting customers to share their experiences and ask questions. This created a feedback loop that was invaluable in product development and marketing. The word-of-mouth marketing that followed was far more effective, and far more authentic, than any paid advertising campaign.

Simultaneously, Samantha tackled the challenge of securing reliable suppliers. Her commitment to sustainability extended beyond the product itself; it permeated her entire supply chain. She spent weeks researching organic farmers and ethically sourced ingredients, building strong relationships with producers who shared her values. She wasn't just looking for the cheapest option; she was searching for partners who could provide consistent quality and transparency. This involved many late nights poring over certifications, comparing prices and logistics, and building trust with potential suppliers who were initially skeptical of a solo entrepreneur from the outback. She meticulously documented every step of the process, creating a detailed system for tracking the provenance of every ingredient, ensuring that the Earth Hues brand remained true to its values. It was a slow, painstaking process, but Samantha knew it was crucial to the long-term success of her business. She wanted to create a transparent and ethical supply chain, one that her customers could trust and one that would stand the test of time.

Building a strong brand identity was another crucial element of her long-term strategy. She recognized that *Earth Hues* was more than just a product; it was a lifestyle, a reflection of her values and her commitment to sustainable living. She worked with a talented graphic designer to create a logo and packaging that perfectly captured this essence – earthy tones, simple lines, and a clear message of natural beauty. She developed a consistent brand voice across all platforms – her website, social media, and even the handwritten notes accompanying her orders. This ensured that the brand's message was clear, consistent, and memorable. She understood that a strong brand identity wasn't just about aesthetics; it was about telling a story, connecting with her customers on an emotional level, and conveying the brand's values and commitment to quality and sustainability. This story was woven into every aspect of her business, from her marketing materials to her customer interactions. It was a narrative that resonated with her target audience, creating a sense of belonging and shared purpose.

Samantha's strategic planning extended beyond the immediate needs of the business. She developed a comprehensive business plan, outlining her short-term and long-term goals, her financial projections, and her marketing strategies. This wasn't just a document for investors; it was a roadmap for her own success. She revisited and updated it regularly, adapting to the changing market dynamics and the evolving needs of her business. This meticulous planning allowed her to anticipate potential challenges and develop contingency plans. She also made conscious choices to reinvest her profits back into the business, focusing on expansion and improvement rather than immediate personal gain. This commitment to long-term growth meant that she prioritized building a sustainable business model over maximizing short-term profits. She understood that building a solid foundation meant being patient, strategic, and willing to prioritize long-term success over instant gratification.

One of the most significant aspects of Samantha's strategic approach was her commitment to continuous learning. She regularly attended industry events, networking with other entrepreneurs and learning from their experiences. She devoured business books and articles, constantly searching for new ideas and strategies to improve her business. She also sought mentorship from experienced business leaders, gaining valuable insights and guidance. This continuous learning kept her business agile, adaptable, and innovative, allowing her to stay ahead of the curve in a rapidly evolving market. It was a constant process of self-improvement and refinement, reflecting her commitment to excellence and her unwavering belief in the potential of her business.

But Samantha's vision extended beyond the confines of her own business. She believed in empowering other women entrepreneurs, particularly those from rural and regional areas. She actively mentored aspiring business owners, sharing her knowledge and experience. She organized workshops and networking events, providing a platform for women to connect, collaborate, and support each other. She understood the challenges of starting a business, especially as a woman, and she was determined to help others navigate those hurdles. This commitment to community and empowerment was not only a personal value; it was also a strategic move to build a strong network of support and collaboration, fostering a supportive ecosystem that benefited everyone involved. This network, built on mutual respect and shared goals, proved invaluable as her business continued to expand.

As the months turned into years, Samantha's careful planning and unwavering dedication began to bear fruit. Her customer base grew steadily, driven by word-of-mouth marketing and her commitment to providing exceptional products and service. Her relationships with suppliers solidified, ensuring a consistent supply of high-quality, ethically sourced ingredients. And her brand identity became synonymous with sustainability, quality, and empowerment. The city lights, once a daunting symbol of her ambition, now reflected the warmth and success of her achievement, a testament to the strength of her vision and the resilience she had cultivated in the quiet solitude of the outback. The foundation was strong, the future was bright, and Samantha, with her team by her side, was ready to take *Earth Hues* to even greater heights. Her journey from outback dreams to city lights was far from over; it was just the beginning of a truly remarkable success story. The initial challenges seemed distant now, replaced by the confidence and assurance of a seasoned entrepreneur who had built not just a business, but a legacy.

CHAPTER 6
Scaling the Business

The air crackled with a different energy now. The sleepy hum of Samantha's initial operation, a cozy cottage industry fueled by late nights and unwavering passion, had been replaced by the frenetic buzz of a rapidly expanding enterprise. Gone were the days of single-handed operations; her once-small team had blossomed, requiring careful cultivation and delegation. The quiet contentment of a manageable workload was replaced by the exhilarating, and sometimes terrifying, rollercoaster of scaling a business. Samantha, ever the pragmatist, embraced the change, understanding that growth, like nature itself, demanded both nurture and calculated risk.

The initial surge had been exhilarating. Orders poured in, exceeding even her most optimistic projections. The positive feedback, the burgeoning customer base – it fueled her ambition, pushing her further, faster. But with this rapid expansion came a whole new set of challenges. The seamless flow of operations, so carefully orchestrated in the beginning, now felt like a chaotic orchestra struggling to find its rhythm. The decisions, once meticulously weighed, now needed to be made at breakneck speed, the weight of responsibility pressing down.

One particularly hectic morning, surrounded by a mountain of paperwork and the cacophony of ringing phones, Samantha felt the familiar pang of self-doubt. Was she truly up to this? Could she manage this whirlwind of growth, maintain the quality, and keep everyone happy? The pressure mounted, threatening to overwhelm her. But as she had done countless times before, Samantha took a deep breath, stepped back, and assessed the situation with her characteristic calm and unwavering resolve. She reminded herself of her core values: quality, integrity, and a commitment to her team. This was not just about profits; it was about building something sustainable, something meaningful.

Recognizing her limitations, Samantha began to delegate tasks, a skill that had not always come naturally. She had previously enjoyed the intimate control of each aspect of the business, but the exponential growth demanded a different approach. She identified key strengths within her team, empowering individuals to take ownership of specific areas. She instituted regular team meetings, fostering open communication and collaborative problem-solving. This wasn't just about dividing the workload; it was about fostering a sense of shared responsibility and collective success. She nurtured talent, providing opportunities for growth and advancement, turning her team into a cohesive unit, each member contributing their unique skills to the overall success.

The transition was not without its hiccups. Initially, some team members struggled to adapt to their new roles and responsibilities. Others found the increased workload challenging. Samantha addressed these issues head-on, providing additional training, mentorship, and clear lines of communication. She established systems and processes to ensure consistency and efficiency, creating a framework for streamlined operations. She learned to trust her team, recognizing their capabilities, and allowing them the space to innovate and excel. It was a gradual process, one that required patience, understanding, and a willingness to adapt her own leadership style.

The expansion also required a significant investment in infrastructure. The small office that had once been sufficient was now bursting at the seams. Samantha secured a larger space, a move that reflected the significant growth of the business. This necessitated new equipment, updated technology, and a whole new level of organizational strategy. The once-simple financial projections needed to be refined and reworked to accommodate the larger scale of operations. She brought in a financial advisor, someone with the expertise to navigate the complex world of finance, securing the stability needed for long-term growth. This was a strategic move that showcased her willingness to seek expert assistance when needed.

As the business grew, Samantha faced the inevitable challenge of adapting to market changes. Consumer preferences shifted, new competitors emerged, and technological advancements threatened to disrupt the established landscape. Samantha, however, met these challenges not with fear, but with a sense of exciting opportunity. She implemented a robust market research strategy, staying abreast of evolving trends and adjusting her offerings to meet changing demands. She fostered a culture of innovation within her team, encouraging experimentation and the exploration of new ideas. This responsiveness to the market, coupled with a willingness to adapt, proved to be crucial in maintaining the business's competitive edge.

The pressure of rapid growth extended beyond the workplace. Samantha found her personal life increasingly encroached upon. The long hours, the constant demands, and the weight of responsibility began to take a toll. She struggled to maintain a healthy work-life balance, a struggle many entrepreneurs can relate to. Her relationships faced strain, her personal time diminished to a precious commodity. Recognizing the importance of self-care, Samantha began to prioritize her well-being. She scheduled regular breaks, ensuring time for exercise, relaxation, and personal pursuits. She actively sought support from family and friends, and sought professional help when the weight of it all became overwhelming. This was a crucial lesson learned: a successful business built on burnout wasn't sustainable.

Through this journey of scaling her business, Samantha learned invaluable lessons in leadership, adaptability, and the importance of a strong team. She discovered that growth wasn't just about expansion; it was about empowerment, both of herself and the people around her. It was about building a culture of collaboration, trust, and shared success. The path was challenging, fraught with uncertainty and unexpected obstacles, but the rewards were immeasurable. Samantha's unwavering dedication, her willingness to learn, and her ability to adapt had transformed a small dream into a thriving enterprise, a testament to the power of resilience, determination, and a steadfast belief in oneself. Her journey was far from over, but she knew that the solid foundation she had built would carry her through the next chapter and beyond. The future, she realised, wasn't something to be feared, but embraced, with the wisdom and strength she had gained along the way.

CHAPTER 7
Strategic Partnerships

The exhilarating growth spurt had left Samantha breathless, but also acutely aware of limitations. Her business, once a charming cottage industry, now needed a wider reach, a stronger voice in the marketplace. Organic growth, while satisfying, simply wasn't enough to fuel the ambitions she now harbored for her company. The solution, she realized, lay in strategic partnerships.

Her initial foray into this world felt like stepping onto a different playing field altogether. It wasn't just about crafting exquisite products anymore; it was about navigating the intricate dance of negotiation, understanding the nuances of different business cultures, and, perhaps most challenging, building trust with individuals she barely knew. Her first potential partner was Amelia Hernandez, owner of a wellestablished online retail platform specializing in ethically sourced goods. Amelia had a considerable online presence, a loyal customer base, and a reputation for impeccable quality —all things Samantha coveted.

Their first meeting took place in a bustling café, the aroma of freshly brewed coffee a stark contrast to the nervous energy humming beneath the surface. Samantha, armed with a meticulously prepared presentation, felt a familiar knot of anxiety tighten in her stomach. She knew Amelia's reputation for being discerning, and the stakes were high. This wasn't just about securing a sales channel; it was about aligning her brand with a company that shared her values. The meeting began with polite pleasantries, a careful exchange of business cards and smiles.

But as the conversation delved into the specifics of a potential collaboration, the true nature of the negotiation began to emerge.

Amelia, direct and to the point, raised concerns about Samantha's production capacity and her ability to meet the demands of a larger customer base. It was a valid concern, one Samantha hadn't fully anticipated. She hadn't just underestimated the scale of the partnership; she had underestimated her own potential to adapt and overcome these challenges. This wasn't just about showcasing her products; it was about demonstrating the resilience of her company and the strength of her team. This initial challenge forced Samantha to confront her limitations head-on, and to actively seek solutions instead of shying away from difficult conversations.

The subsequent weeks were a whirlwind of emails, conference calls, and countless revisions of the partnership agreement. Samantha learned to navigate the delicate balance between asserting her company's value and being receptive to Amelia's concerns. She discovered the power of active listening, understanding that a successful partnership wasn't about winning a negotiation, but about finding common ground and building a mutually beneficial relationship. The process tested her patience, stretched her negotiating skills, and demanded a level of flexibility she hadn't previously known she possessed. But she persevered, driven by the vision of what this partnership could achieve for her company.

Finally, after weeks of intense negotiations, the contract was signed. A wave of relief washed over Samantha, followed by the exhilarating realization that she had accomplished something truly significant. The partnership with Amelia opened doors she had only dreamed of. Her products were now showcased prominently on Amelia's website, reaching a significantly wider audience and generating a surge in sales. The collaboration also brought unexpected benefits: Amelia's team offered valuable insights into online marketing strategies, and Samantha's team contributed their unique expertise in product design and ethical sourcing. It was a mutually enriching exchange, a testament to the power of collaboration.

Her success with Amelia fueled her confidence to pursue other strategic partnerships. She reached out to a local artisan collective, a group of talented individuals who shared her passion for sustainable practices. This partnership proved to be a different kind of challenge. The collective operated on a more informal basis, with a strong emphasis on community and shared decision-making. Negotiating with a group instead of a single individual proved complex, requiring Samantha to adapt her communication style and approach to consensus-building. This experience highlighted the importance of understanding different organizational cultures and adapting one's strategies accordingly. She learned the value of patience, compromise, and collaborative decision-making. The collective's artisan skills complemented her products, adding unique and valuable features to her offerings, further enhancing her brand's appeal.

Another partnership emerged with a prominent social media influencer, known for her commitment to ethical and sustainable living. This collaboration focused on brand awareness and targeted marketing. The influencer, Chloe, had a massive online following, particularly among Samantha's target demographic. Working with Chloe required a different set of skills: understanding the nuances of social media marketing, content creation, and managing the complexities of influencer marketing campaigns. This collaboration was less about formal contracts and more about building a genuine relationship based on mutual respect and shared values. The results were remarkable; Chloe's engaging content and vast reach propelled Samantha's brand into the spotlight, creating a significant buzz and driving substantial sales growth.

Through these experiences, Samantha learned that strategic partnerships weren't simply about securing sales channels or expanding market reach. They were about building relationships, forging connections, and creating a network of support and collaboration. She discovered the importance of identifying the right partners – individuals or organizations that shared her values, complemented her strengths, and possessed the resources and expertise to enhance her business. This was not just about transactional relationships; it was about fostering genuine connections that led to mutual growth and success. The process demanded constant learning, adaptation, and the development of strong communication and negotiation skills.

The journey wasn't without its setbacks. Not every partnership proved successful. Some collaborations fizzled out due to conflicting visions, misaligned expectations, or unforeseen challenges. These experiences, while initially disappointing, proved invaluable learning opportunities. Samantha learned to identify red flags early on, to be more discerning in selecting partners, and to have a clear exit strategy in place. She understood that not every partnership is meant to last, and that failure, in this context, was not an indicator of personal or professional inadequacy but an opportunity for growth and refinement.

These strategic alliances significantly reshaped Samantha's business. They not only boosted sales and market share but also enhanced her brand's reputation, broadened her network, and provided access to valuable expertise and resources.

More importantly, however, these partnerships reflected Samantha's growth as a business leader. She had evolved from a solo entrepreneur operating in relative isolation to a strategic thinker, adept at building relationships, negotiating deals, and collaborating effectively with diverse individuals and organizations. She embraced the complexity, the challenges, and the inherent risks involved, understanding that the rewards – both personal and professional – far outweighed the uncertainties. The journey had been demanding, but the results were a testament to the power of strategic partnerships and the visionary leadership that brought them to fruition. The future, once a daunting prospect, now looked brighter, more expansive, and filled with exciting possibilities.

CHAPTER 8
Overcoming Competition

The initial euphoria of her successful partnerships began to fade as Samantha found herself staring down the barrel of a rapidly intensifying competitive landscape. Her oncecomfortable niche in the artisanal soap market was now teeming with imitators, each vying for a piece of the pie she had so diligently baked. The charming, hand-painted labels that had once set her apart were now being replicated, sometimes even surpassed, by slicker, more modern designs. The delightful, evocative scents she had painstakingly developed were being mimicked, their unique formulas subtly altered to skirt the edges of copyright protection. The sense of being overwhelmed was palpable.

Samantha's first instinct was to react defensively. She considered legal action, a protracted and expensive battle she wasn't sure she could win. The sheer number of competitors, many operating on smaller margins and with less overhead, made a comprehensive legal campaign impractical. Then there was the question of negative publicity. A drawn-out lawsuit, even if successful, could tarnish her brand's image and alienate her loyal customer base.

Instead, Samantha took a deep breath and decided to analyze the situation strategically. She assembled her team—a small, but fiercely loyal group—and together they conducted a thorough competitive analysis. They studied their competitors' pricing strategies, marketing campaigns, distribution channels, and product lines. They scrutinized customer reviews, paying close attention to both praise and criticism. They identified strengths and weaknesses, opportunities and threats, not just for their own company, but for each of their key competitors as well.

The analysis revealed a clear pattern. Many of her competitors were focusing on low-cost, mass-produced soaps, sacrificing quality and uniqueness for sheer volume. Others were trying to emulate her success with artisanal products, but lacked the attention to detail and the passion that had fueled her own growth. Still others were targeting niche markets, focusing on specific scents, ingredients, or consumer demographics.

Samantha recognized an opportunity. She realized that while some consumers were drawn to inexpensive alternatives, many others were willing to pay a premium for high-quality, ethically sourced, and uniquely crafted soaps. This was her target market – the discerning consumer who appreciated artistry, sustainability, and authenticity.

To solidify her position in this market, Samantha decided to double down on what made her brand unique. She invested in even higher-quality ingredients, sourcing them directly from local farmers and cooperatives. She collaborated with a renowned graphic designer to create a new, more sophisticated brand identity that reflected the elegance and sophistication of her products. She also revamped her packaging, using sustainable and recyclable materials that appealed to her environmentally conscious customer base.

But the most significant change involved her marketing strategy. She shifted away from mass-market advertising and instead focused on building deeper relationships with her customers. She started a blog where she shared her passion for natural ingredients, soap-making techniques, and sustainable business practices. She hosted workshops and online classes, teaching her customers how to make their own soap and connecting with them on a personal level. She actively engaged with her social media followers, answering questions, sharing behind-the-scenes glimpses of her work, and fostering a sense of community around her brand.

This personalized approach not only helped to distinguish her products from the mass-produced alternatives but also fostered a sense of loyalty and brand advocacy among her customers. Word-of-mouth marketing became a powerful engine of growth, surpassing the reach of traditional advertising campaigns. She also started a loyalty program rewarding frequent customers, further enhancing their experience and encouraging repeat purchases.

Samantha also identified another underserved area – customized soaps. Recognizing that customers appreciated the personalization aspect, she introduced a range of bespoke options, allowing customers to select their preferred scents, ingredients, and even customize the packaging. This personalized touch made her products stand out from the generic offerings of her competitors.

Furthermore, Samantha decided to expand her product line beyond soaps. She introduced a range of complementary products, such as lotions, bath bombs, and shower gels, all made with the same high-quality ingredients and commitment to sustainability. This expansion allowed her to cater to a broader range of customer needs and increased her overall revenue streams. The careful branding and messaging emphasized the holistic experience, seamlessly tying all products together with her core ethos of natural, sustainable beauty.

Her competitors were caught off guard. They had expected a straightforward price war or a battle for shelf space, but Samantha's strategic maneuvers were far more nuanced. Her approach wasn't about undercutting the competition; it was about outsmarting them, creating a brand that was synonymous with quality, authenticity, and a unique customer experience.

The investment in high-quality ingredients and sophisticated packaging did increase her production costs, but the higher price point was justified by the superior quality and the unique brand experience she was creating. This strategy proved extremely effective, attracting customers who were willing to pay more for a product they perceived as superior in quality and value.

The response from the market was overwhelmingly positive. Her sales continued to grow, exceeding even her most optimistic projections. She had not only weathered the storm of increased competition but had emerged stronger, more resilient, and more innovative than ever before. The experience had been a powerful lesson in the importance of adaptability, strategic thinking, and the cultivation of a loyal customer base.

Samantha's journey served as a powerful testament to the idea that true success in business isn't just about outspending or out-marketing the competition. It's about understanding the nuances of the market, identifying underserved needs, and creating a brand that resonates deeply with its customers. Her story became an inspiring example of how a small business could not only survive but thrive in a fiercely competitive environment by focusing on its core strengths, innovating consistently, and building a strong, loyal community around its brand. The competitive landscape, once a source of anxiety, had become a proving ground for her creativity, resilience, and strategic brilliance. It confirmed that true success wasn't merely about avoiding competition but about creatively navigating it. The future, once clouded with uncertainty, now shimmered with the promise of continued growth and innovation. The challenges she had faced, far from diminishing her spirit, had forged her into an even more formidable entrepreneur, ready to meet whatever the market threw her way. And she knew, with unwavering confidence, that she would meet each challenge with the same ingenuity, resilience, and unwavering belief in her vision. The journey was far from over, but Samantha was ready. The competitive arena had become her stage, and she was ready for her encore. The future was hers for the taking, a testament to her relentless pursuit of excellence and her refusal to be defined by the limitations others perceived.

CHAPTER 9
Maintaining Work-Life Balance

The scent of lavender and chamomile, usually a comforting balm, now felt suffocating. Samantha, surrounded by the fragrant chaos of her burgeoning soap empire, felt a deep, gnawing exhaustion. The relentless pace of growth, the constant pressure to innovate, to outmaneuver competitors, had taken its toll. She'd poured every ounce of her energy, every fiber of her being, into building her brand, sacrificing almost everything else in the process.

Her once vibrant social life had dwindled to a handful of hurried lunches and even more hurried phone calls. Weekends, once filled with hikes in the nearby mountains and leisurely brunches with friends, were now consumed by inventory checks, marketing strategies, and the endless cycle of emails and meetings. The close relationship she'd once shared with her sister, Sarah, had become strained; the distance, both physical and emotional, felt vast and unbridgeable. Sarah's gentle reminders to "slow down, Sam," were met with a defensive, almost brittle, response. She felt guilty, yes, but the guilt was overshadowed by the relentless pressure to succeed, to prove herself, to maintain the momentum she'd so painstakingly built.

The apartment, once a haven of calm and creativity, now felt more like a storage unit for soap supplies. Stacks of packaging materials overflowed from corners, and the sweet, cloying scent of her creations hung heavy in the air, a constant reminder of the work that never seemed to end. Sleep became a luxury she could rarely afford, often sacrificing precious hours to catch up on emails or brainstorm new product ideas. Evenings were spent hunched over spreadsheets, the glow of her laptop illuminating her tired face.

The physical toll was undeniable. Samantha's once healthy complexion was now marred by dark circles under her eyes, a testament to countless sleepless nights. Headaches were a constant companion, a throbbing reminder of the relentless stress. She found herself increasingly irritable, snapping at colleagues and even her beloved dog, Barnaby, whose unwavering loyalty remained a silent comfort amidst the storm.

One particularly grueling week, after a series of back-toback meetings and a disastrous product launch that threatened to unravel months of meticulous work, Samantha collapsed. The exhaustion finally caught up to her, leaving her weak and vulnerable. Lying in bed, the weight of her responsibilities pressing down on her, she realized she was at a breaking point. This wasn't sustainable. She was burning the candle at both ends, consuming herself in the relentless pursuit of success, neglecting the very things that nourished her soul and kept her thriving.

The realization hit her with the force of a tidal wave. She couldn't continue down this path. Her ambition, once a driving force, had become a destructive one, eroding her well-being and threatening to shatter the very foundation she had so diligently built. She knew she needed to make a change, to recalibrate her approach, and to prioritize her own well-being. But how?

The answer, she realized, wasn't about abandoning her ambitions but about integrating them into a more balanced and sustainable lifestyle. It was about learning to say "no" to projects that didn't align with her priorities, and to delegate tasks that didn't require her direct involvement. It meant actively seeking support from her team, acknowledging her limitations, and trusting others to share the workload.

Samantha began by scheduling regular breaks throughout her day. She started with short, five-minute meditation sessions, using a guided meditation app on her phone. These brief moments of stillness helped to center her, allowing her to clear her mind and approach challenges with renewed focus. She also incorporated short walks around the block during her lunch break, using the fresh air and physical activity to combat the effects of prolonged sitting.

Next, she consciously prioritized her relationships. She scheduled regular phone calls with her sister, Sarah, and made a point of having dinner with friends once a week. These connections, she realized, were crucial to her wellbeing. The simple act of sharing a meal, a laugh, or a heartfelt conversation rekindled her sense of belonging and restored her perspective.

She also rediscovered her love of hiking, resuming her weekend trips to the mountains, albeit with a smaller, more manageable itinerary. These excursions weren't just about physical activity; they were opportunities for solitude, reflection, and reconnection with nature. The quiet beauty of the mountains offered a stark contrast to the frenetic energy of her work life, a much-needed respite that allowed her to recharge and replenish her creative wellspring.

Samantha also invested in professional help. She began seeing a therapist, who helped her manage stress, identify unhealthy coping mechanisms, and develop strategies for setting boundaries and delegating tasks more effectively. The therapist helped her to understand that prioritizing self-care wasn't selfish, but essential for her long-term well-being and the success of her business.

She implemented a strict "no-work" policy on weekends, a rule she found herself initially struggling to adhere to. But as she began to experience the benefits of disconnecting from work, the temptation to check emails or work on projects diminished. She rediscovered the simple joys of life:

spending quality time with Barnaby, curling up with a good book, or simply enjoying a quiet evening at home.

The transition wasn't easy. There were moments of doubt, moments when the old habits threatened to reassert themselves. But Samantha's unwavering commitment to her well-being kept her focused on her goals. She learned to forgive herself when she stumbled, and she celebrated the small victories along the way.

The changes she made weren't just about improving her personal well-being; they also had a positive impact on her business. By prioritizing her mental and physical health, Samantha was better able to handle the pressures of her work. She became more productive, more creative, and more effective in her decision-making. Her improved well-being translated into improved leadership, fostering a healthier and more productive work environment for her team. The balance she had so diligently sought allowed her to approach challenges with renewed energy and resilience. Her soap business continued to flourish, not at the cost of her wellbeing, but in harmony with it. Samantha's story became a powerful example of how a balanced approach to life and work could lead to both personal and professional fulfillment. The future, once a blur of relentless activity, now held the promise of sustained success, achieved not through relentless striving, but through mindful intention and a commitment to holistic well-being. She'd learned that success, truly, wasn't a destination, but a journey, one best traveled with a balanced heart and a clear mind. And Samantha, finally, was ready for the next chapter, knowing she had the tools and the wisdom to navigate it with grace, resilience, and a renewed sense of purpose.

CHAPTER 10
Giving Back to the Community

The lavender fields surrounding her childhood home held a different scent now, a scent less of fragrant blooms and more of possibility. Samantha, leaning against the weathered wooden fence, felt a profound shift within her. The relentless drive that had fueled her soap empire's meteoric rise had mellowed, replaced by a quiet contentment tinged with a burgeoning sense of responsibility. She'd built something remarkable, but what was the point of success if it didn't extend beyond the bottom line?

This realization had sparked a fire within her, a desire to give back to the community that had nurtured her dreams. It wasn't a sudden, impulsive decision; it was a slow, deliberate unfolding, a natural consequence of her newfound equilibrium. She had learned the hard way that a life solely focused on professional achievement left a hollowness at its core. Now, she was determined to fill that void with meaningful contributions, to use her success as a catalyst for positive change.

Her first initiative was remarkably simple yet profoundly impactful: a mentorship program for young women in her town. She remembered the struggles she'd faced, the moments of self-doubt, the lack of guidance that had nearly derailed her ambitions. She wouldn't let other young women face the same challenges alone. She partnered with the local high school, offering workshops on entrepreneurship, business planning, and financial literacy. These weren't dry, theoretical sessions; they were interactive, hands-on experiences, filled with real-world examples and inspiring stories from her own journey. She shared her mistakes, her triumphs, and the invaluable lessons learned along the way, fostering an environment of open communication and mutual support.

The response was overwhelming. Girls who had previously felt lost and uncertain discovered a newfound confidence, a sense of agency they hadn't known they possessed. Samantha witnessed their transformations firsthand, the shy whispers morphing into confident declarations, the hesitant steps evolving into determined strides. She saw reflections of her younger self in their eyes, a spark of potential waiting to ignite. She established a scholarship fund, providing financial assistance to deserving students pursuing their educational goals, helping to break down the barriers that often prevented talented young women from achieving their full potential. The fund went beyond tuition fees; it encompassed materials, mentorship, and even modest living stipends to ease the financial burden many students faced.

Beyond the mentorship program, Samantha channeled her resources into supporting local charities. She made substantial donations to the community center, funding afterschool programs that focused on arts, technology, and leadership development. She spearheaded a fundraising campaign for the local animal shelter, a cause close to her heart, organizing a charity soap-making event that brought the entire community together. The event was a resounding success, raising thousands of dollars and bringing awareness to the plight of abandoned animals. This initiative went beyond mere financial support; it involved her actively volunteering at the shelter, spending weekends cuddling kittens and walking dogs, finding solace and unexpected joy in the process.

Her philanthropy wasn't limited to monetary contributions. She recognized the power of her brand, her soap empire, as a force for good. She launched a line of ethically sourced, sustainably produced soaps, using only organic ingredients and employing fair-trade practices. The packaging itself was eco-friendly, reflecting her commitment to environmental responsibility. A portion of the proceeds from this line was donated directly to environmental conservation organizations, supporting reforestation efforts and protecting endangered species. She created a marketing campaign that highlighted not only the quality of her products but also the ethical principles underpinning her business. This resonated deeply with customers who valued transparency and social responsibility, further boosting her brand's reputation and allowing her to give even more back to the planet.

Samantha's commitment extended to supporting small businesses within her community. She understood the struggles of entrepreneurs firsthand, the constant hurdles and challenges they faced. She established a business incubator program, offering guidance, resources, and mentorship to aspiring entrepreneurs, particularly women and minorityowned businesses. She shared her expertise in marketing, finance, and operations, providing them with the tools and support they needed to flourish. She didn't view them as competitors but as collaborators, believing in the power of collective growth and mutual support. She organized networking events, connecting small businesses with potential investors and partners, fostering a vibrant ecosystem of entrepreneurship within the community.

Her efforts went beyond the immediate vicinity of her hometown. She partnered with international organizations focused on women's empowerment, donating a percentage of her profits to support their initiatives. She traveled to developing countries, witnessing firsthand the impact of her contributions and forging a deeper understanding of the challenges faced by women in different parts of the world. These experiences profoundly shaped her perspective, reaffirming her commitment to global social responsibility. She shared these experiences through her social media platforms, raising awareness and encouraging others to join her in making a difference.

Her giving wasn't just about writing checks or launching initiatives; it was about personal involvement. She regularly volunteered at soup kitchens, spent time mentoring children at after-school programs, and participated in community clean-up initiatives. She embraced the simple act of showing up, of lending a hand, of being present in the lives of those around her. It was a fundamental shift in her mindset, a move away from solely focusing on individual achievement towards embracing collective well-being.

The transformation wasn't merely about philanthropy; it was about reclaiming her roots. The lavender fields, once a nostalgic backdrop to her childhood, now represented a renewed connection to her community, a sense of belonging that transcended personal ambition. Her success wasn't a solitary achievement but a shared victory, a testament to the support she had received and the responsibility she felt to give back. The fragrance of lavender, once suffocating, now held a different, more profound scent – the sweet aroma of purpose, fulfillment, and a life lived with intention. Samantha, once driven by the relentless pursuit of success, now found a deeper, more enduring satisfaction in the ripple effect of her generosity, in the positive change she was creating, not only for her own life but for the lives of others. The future held not only the promise of continued business success but also the enduring satisfaction of a life dedicated to making a difference, one act of kindness, one philanthropic endeavor, one empowered individual at a time. The journey, she realized, was just as important, if not more so, than the destination, and she was finally traveling it with a heart full of gratitude and a soul brimming with purpose.

CHAPTER 11
Financial Crisis

———◦꒰ ꒱◦———

The air in Samantha's office crackled with tension. Not the usual, productive tension of a busy workday, but a suffocating, anxiety-inducing pressure that threatened to crush everything she'd built. The global financial crisis, which had initially seemed a distant rumble on the horizon, had arrived with the force of a tsunami, washing away the comfortable stability she'd carefully cultivated. Her usually meticulously organized desk was a chaotic mess, overflowing with financial reports, emails, and the lingering scent of stale coffee. The once vibrant, optimistic atmosphere of her company was now replaced with a palpable unease, the hushed whispers of worried employees a constant reminder of the precarious situation.

The market had plummeted. Investors, once eager to pour money into her innovative company, were now hesitant, their confidence shaken by the economic downturn. Samantha stared at the latest financial projections, a knot tightening in her stomach. The numbers painted a grim picture, starkly contrasting with the vibrant success of the past few years. Her meticulously crafted business plan, her carefully calculated risk assessments – all seemed irrelevant in the face of this unprecedented crisis. She'd faced challenges before, weathered storms of doubt and setbacks, but this felt different. This felt existential.

Days bled into nights. Samantha found herself working longer hours than ever before, fueled by adrenaline and an unwavering refusal to surrender. Sleep became a luxury she could barely afford, her mind racing even in the brief moments of rest. She'd always prided herself on her rational approach to business, on her ability to analyze data and make strategic decisions. But now, emotion was a powerful force, threatening to overwhelm her calculated responses. Fear gnawed at the edges of her resolve, whispering doubts and anxieties that threatened to consume her.

She called emergency meetings, her voice strained but determined, addressing her team with a mix of honesty and reassurance. She laid out the facts, acknowledging the severity of the situation without succumbing to panic. She emphasized the importance of teamwork, of collaboration, of pulling together to navigate these turbulent waters. She rallied her employees, reminding them of their shared vision, their collective strength, and the resilience they'd displayed time and time again.

The response from her team was immediate and powerful. Her employees, many of whom had been with her since the beginning, understood the gravity of the situation but also understood her leadership and unwavering commitment. They responded with renewed dedication, their energy fueling her own resolve. They weren't just employees; they were partners, invested in the success of the company as much as she was. The collective energy in the office, although still tense, was now infused with a sense of unity and shared purpose.

Samantha's strategic thinking was paramount during this crisis. She immediately implemented cost-cutting measures, streamlining operations, negotiating better deals with suppliers, and prioritizing essential projects. She meticulously reviewed every expense, searching for areas to trim without sacrificing the quality of her products or services. She made tough decisions, some painful, but necessary for the survival of her business. She knew that short-term pain could potentially lead to long-term gain.

Simultaneously, she focused on securing new funding. She reached out to existing investors, presenting them with a revised business plan, highlighting the company's strengths, its resilience, and its potential for growth even within this challenging climate. She attended industry events, networking with potential investors, her pitch refined and focused, her conviction unwavering. She didn't shy away from the challenges, instead presenting them as opportunities for strategic investment, emphasizing the potential for high returns once the market stabilized.

She also explored alternative funding avenues. She considered government grants, exploring various programs designed to support small businesses during economic downturns. She researched crowdfunding options, considering the potential for engaging her loyal customer base directly. Every avenue, every possibility, was explored with the tenacity and determination that had always been her hallmark.

The process was agonizingly slow. Rejections piled up, each one a fresh blow to her confidence. There were days when the weight of the responsibility threatened to overwhelm her, days when the doubt crept in, whispering insidious suggestions of surrender. But Samantha refused to yield. She drew strength from her team, from her unwavering belief in her vision, and from the memories of her past successes. She knew that giving up wasn't an option; she had too much invested, too much at stake, not only for herself but for the people who believed in her, who depended on her.

The turning point came unexpectedly. A prominent venture capitalist, initially hesitant due to the market's instability, saw something in Samantha's unwavering resolve, in her strategic thinking, in her ability to navigate the crisis with such grace and determination. He recognized the underlying strength of her business model, its resilience, and its potential for explosive growth once the storm passed. He agreed to invest, a lifeline that injected much-needed capital into the company.

The investment was a game-changer. It provided the breathing room Samantha desperately needed, allowing her to weather the storm and emerge stronger than ever. The company didn't just survive; it thrived. The crisis had tested her to her limits, pushing her to make difficult decisions, to confront her fears, and to dig deep for resources she didn't know she possessed. But it had also refined her, honed her skills, and strengthened her resolve. She had emerged from the ashes, not just intact, but transformed, a stronger, more resilient entrepreneur, her business a testament to her unwavering grit and strategic brilliance. The experience would forever shape her understanding of leadership, risk management, and the importance of never giving up, even when the odds seemed insurmountable. The financial crisis had been a crucible, and Samantha had emerged forged in the fires of adversity, a beacon of strength and inspiration.

CHAPTER 12
Unexpected Setbacks

The initial euphoria of securing the investment faded as quickly as the morning mist. Samantha, still reeling from the near-death experience of the financial crisis, found herself facing a new set of challenges, ones that were far more insidious and less predictable than the global economic downturn. The first blow came in the form of a key employee's sudden resignation. Sarah, her head of marketing, a woman who had been instrumental in building the company's brand and driving sales, had accepted a lucrative offer from a competitor. The news hit Samantha like a punch to the gut. Sarah wasn't just a talented marketer; she was a confidante, a friend, a crucial part of Samantha's inner circle. Losing her was a personal blow as much as a professional one.

The void left by Sarah was substantial. Marketing campaigns stalled, deadlines were missed, and the carefully constructed marketing strategy began to unravel. Samantha, accustomed to handling pressure, found herself overwhelmed. The efficient, decisive leader she had become during the crisis seemed to falter, replaced by a wave of self-doubt. She struggled to fill Sarah's shoes, juggling her own responsibilities with the added burden of overseeing the marketing department. The pressure mounted, leading to sleepless nights and an unhealthy reliance on caffeine. She felt the familiar tightening in her chest, the precursor to the anxiety attacks that had plagued her in the darkest days of the financial crisis.

This time, however, Samantha approached the situation differently. She didn't allow the self-doubt to consume her. Instead, she acknowledged her limitations, a significant shift from her previous tendency to shoulder every burden alone. She realized the importance of delegating effectively, a lesson learned the hard way. She sought out the support of her remaining team members, empowering them to take on greater responsibility and fostering a collaborative environment. She hired a temporary consultant to help bridge the gap, providing valuable mentorship and training to her team.

The second unexpected setback arrived in the form of a critical product recall. A minor manufacturing flaw, unnoticed during quality control, resulted in a batch of their flagship product malfunctioning. The news spread like wildfire, causing a public relations nightmare. The initial reaction was panic. Customers demanded refunds, the media amplified the issue, and the company's reputation was tarnished. The financial implications were severe, threatening to erase the gains made during the recovery from the financial crisis.

This time, Samantha's response was swift and decisive. She immediately activated the company's crisis management plan, a comprehensive strategy developed after the lessons learned from the financial crisis. Transparency became her guiding principle. Instead of trying to bury the issue, Samantha publicly acknowledged the problem, taking full responsibility and outlining the steps being taken to rectify the situation. She offered full refunds and replacements, exceeding customer expectations to demonstrate her commitment to their satisfaction.

This proactive approach, coupled with a heartfelt apology, proved remarkably effective. While the initial damage was substantial, the company's honest and decisive response mitigated the fallout. Customers appreciated the transparency and the company's commitment to resolving the issue, and the media coverage shifted from outrage to admiration. The crisis, while undeniably painful, highlighted the importance of having a robust crisis management plan in place and the power of genuine remorse and transparent communication.

The challenges didn't end there. The competitive landscape shifted dramatically, with new players emerging and established companies aggressively vying for market share. Samantha found herself navigating a landscape that was constantly evolving, adapting to new technologies, and anticipating shifts in consumer demand. She realized the importance of continuous learning and adaptation, a crucial element for survival in a rapidly changing market. She invested in professional development for her team, encouraging them to explore new technologies and develop innovative solutions. She embraced experimentation, launching pilot programs to test new products and services, and she wasn't afraid to fail, viewing failures as valuable learning opportunities.

She discovered the power of networking, actively seeking out mentors and advisors who could provide valuable insights and guidance. She participated in industry conferences and events, building relationships with other entrepreneurs and learning from their experiences. She embraced collaboration, seeking out partnerships with complementary businesses to expand her reach and offer more comprehensive solutions to her customers.

Through these unexpected setbacks, Samantha discovered a resilience she didn't know she possessed. She learned that setbacks were not failures, but rather opportunities for growth and learning. They forced her to adapt, innovate, and refine her strategies. She developed a deeper understanding of leadership, risk management, and the importance of building strong teams. She embraced change as an inevitability, viewing it not as a threat but as an opportunity for progress. She discovered the importance of prioritizing her own well-being, recognizing that burnout was not a sign of weakness but a symptom of neglecting self-care.

She implemented strategies for maintaining a healthy worklife balance, incorporating regular exercise, mindfulness practices, and time for personal pursuits into her daily routine. She cultivated strong relationships with her family and friends, recognizing that their support was essential for navigating the challenges of entrepreneurship. She understood that success wasn't just about achieving financial goals, but about building a fulfilling life that encompassed personal well-being and meaningful relationships.

The journey had been far from easy. The setbacks had tested her resolve, pushed her to her limits, and challenged her assumptions. But in overcoming these challenges, Samantha had not only strengthened her business, but also transformed herself. She had emerged not just as a successful entrepreneur, but as a leader, a mentor, and a resilient woman who had found her strength in the face of adversity. The unexpected setbacks had been unexpected opportunities for growth, and she realized that the most valuable lessons she learned weren't from her triumphs, but from her struggles. It was in the face of adversity that she had truly discovered her strength, resilience, and unwavering determination. The path ahead remained uncertain, filled with potential obstacles and challenges. But armed with the wisdom gained from her experiences, Samantha knew she could face whatever came her way, ready to learn, adapt, and thrive. The unexpected setbacks hadn't broken her; they had made her stronger. They had forged her into the leader she was always meant to be.

CHAPTER 13
Personal Sacrifices

The quiet hum of the city outside faded into the background as Samantha sat at her kitchen table, a half-empty cup of chamomile tea growing cold beside her. The sleek, modern apartment, a testament to her professional success, felt strangely empty. The vibrant energy that usually thrummed through her veins had been replaced by a quiet exhaustion, a weariness that settled deep in her bones. Sarah's departure still echoed in her mind, a constant, low thrum of loss. It wasn't just the professional setback; it was the personal one that gnawed at her. Sarah had been more than an employee; she had been a friend, a confidante, someone who understood the unique pressures and anxieties of building a business from the ground up.

Losing Sarah felt like a severing, a fracture in the already delicate balance of her life. She'd poured so much into her company, her every waking thought consumed by spreadsheets, strategies, and sales figures. The relentless pursuit of success had become a singular focus, eclipsing almost everything else. And now, staring at the reflection of the city lights in her teacup, she saw the cost.

She thought of her parents, their calls growing less frequent, their voices tinged with a subtle disappointment that she rarely seemed to have time for them. The last family holiday had been a rushed affair, squeezed between investor meetings and product launches. The guilt was a heavy cloak, wrapping itself around her shoulders, stifling her breath. She pictured her father's kind eyes, the lines etched by years of hard work and quiet pride, a pride that felt tainted by her absence. She remembered her mother's gentle smile, always ready with words of encouragement, but now shadowed by a quiet concern she couldn't quite dismiss. She owed them so much more.

Then there was Mark, her long-term boyfriend, a man who had patiently supported her through the thick and thin of her entrepreneurial journey. He'd celebrated every milestone with her, offered comfort during the inevitable setbacks, and absorbed the emotional fallout of her relentless ambition. But lately, she realized with a pang of regret, she'd taken him for granted. Their dates were infrequent, often replaced by late-night work sessions and early morning calls. She'd lost the art of simply being present, of putting her phone down and truly connecting with him. His gentle understanding had turned into quiet acceptance, a subtle shift that spoke volumes about the toll her ambition had taken on their relationship.

The unspoken tensions had been building for months, a slow simmering resentment that threatened to boil over. She remembered the last time they'd had a proper conversation, a rare evening out punctuated by stilted silence and forced smiles. He'd talked about his own ambitions, his own dreams, dreams that had been overshadowed by her relentless pursuit of hers. His words now echoed in her ears, a painful reminder of her self-absorption. He hadn't voiced anger, but a profound sadness hung in the air between them, a sadness that mirrored her own.

Sleepless nights were becoming the norm, filled with the unsettling realization that she'd built a successful business at the expense of her personal life. The price of success, she realized with a sobering clarity, had been steep. The rewards had been tangible, visible in the sleek lines of her office, the impressive figures on her financial statements. But the losses were intangible, woven into the fabric of her relationships, the subtle fissures in the bonds she cherished. The weight of this realization settled heavily upon her.

She'd always been driven, a relentless pursuer of her goals, a woman who refused to accept limitations. This ambition, this unwavering determination, had been both her strength and her weakness. It had propelled her forward, allowed her to overcome seemingly insurmountable obstacles. Yet, in its shadow, it had cast a pall over her personal life, leaving her feeling isolated, disconnected, and profoundly lonely despite her outward success.

The following week was a blur of conciliatory calls and desperate attempts to rebuild bridges. She arranged a family dinner, a proper one, at her parents' house, a gesture that was as much for her as it was for them. She surprised them with their favorite Italian food, engaged in long, meaningful conversations, and listened more than she spoke. She spent that evening soaking in the quiet comfort of their company, feeling the weight of her guilt slowly begin to lift.

With Mark, she initiated a deeper, more honest conversation, revealing her vulnerability and acknowledging her shortcomings. She spoke of her fears, her regrets, her profound need to find a balance between her ambition and her personal life. It was a difficult conversation, fraught with unspoken resentments and raw emotion. But it was also a liberating one, a step towards restoring the connection that had been strained and frayed. He listened, his eyes filled with a mixture of understanding and a hint of hope. The conversation wasn't a magical fix; it was a beginning, a crucial first step in rebuilding a fractured relationship.

Samantha's journey to rectify the damage wouldn't be quick or easy. It demanded constant vigilance, a conscious effort to prioritize relationships alongside professional success. She began small, scheduling regular date nights, making time for family dinners, and consciously disconnecting from work after a certain hour. She started delegating more effectively, empowering her team to take on greater responsibility, allowing herself to step back and focus on aspects of her life that had been neglected for so long.

The change wasn't immediate, nor was it always smooth. The pull towards her work remained strong, a powerful force that threatened to derail her efforts. There were days when she slipped back into old habits, losing herself in the demands of her business. But each time, she caught herself, reminding herself of the sacrifices she'd made and the price she'd paid. These missteps, however, served as reminders of the ongoing commitment she needed to make, a commitment to balance, to integration, to building a life that encompassed both her ambition and her heart.

The process of reconciliation was a slow, gradual unfolding, a journey that demanded self-awareness, introspection, and a willingness to confront her own flaws. It required her to acknowledge the shortcomings of her relentless ambition, to see its shadow side, and to actively work toward finding a more sustainable, fulfilling way to live. She started journaling, a way to process her emotions, to understand the root of her actions, and to articulate her goals more clearly. She discovered a renewed appreciation for the simple joys of life, the comfort of family, the intimacy of a loving relationship, things that had been obscured by the relentless pursuit of professional success.

The transformation wasn't just about regaining what she'd lost. It was about becoming a more complete, more balanced individual, a woman who understood the importance of integrating her professional aspirations with her personal life. It was a lesson learned the hard way, a lesson etched in the heart by the scars of neglect and the sweetness of rediscovered connection. The journey was far from over, but Samantha now possessed a clearer vision, a more holistic understanding of what true success entailed, and a newfound determination to achieve a life that was rich in both achievement and love. The path ahead would still present challenges, but Samantha knew, deep within her, that she was now better equipped to navigate them, not just as a successful entrepreneur, but as a whole person, finally integrating the pieces of her life that had been so long fractured and separated.

CHAPTER 14
Mentorship and Guidance

The following weeks were a blur of activity, a whirlwind of strategizing, networking, and soul-searching. Samantha, fueled by a newfound resolve, immersed herself in rebuilding her team and re-evaluating her business strategies. But even amidst the chaos of re-establishing her company, she knew she couldn't do it alone. The loneliness she'd felt in the aftermath of Sarah's departure had been a stark reminder of the importance of mentorship and guidance. She reached out to Isabella Rossi, a titan in the tech industry whose name was synonymous with innovation and resilience. Isabella, known for her sharp intellect and unwavering support of female entrepreneurs, had been an inspiration to Samantha for years.

The meeting took place in Isabella's minimalist office, a space that reflected her powerful, yet understated personality. Sunlight streamed through the panoramic windows, illuminating the cityscape below. Isabella, with her silver-streaked hair pulled back in a sleek ponytail and a warm smile that instantly put Samantha at ease, offered her a cup of strong Italian espresso. The conversation flowed easily, a blend of professional insight and personal encouragement. Isabella listened intently as Samantha recounted her experiences, the challenges, and the lessons learned. She didn't offer easy answers or platitudes; instead, she asked insightful questions, challenging Samantha's assumptions and pushing her to think critically about her approach.

"Samantha," Isabella said, her voice calm and measured, "building a successful business is a marathon, not a sprint.

There will be setbacks, there will be losses. The key is to learn from them, to adapt, and to keep moving forward. You've shown resilience; that's a powerful asset. But resilience alone isn't enough. You need a strong support system, a network of mentors, advisors, and friends who can offer guidance and encouragement when you need it most." Isabella's words resonated deeply with Samantha. She'd been so focused on proving herself, on achieving success on her own terms, that she'd neglected the importance of collaboration and community.

Isabella's mentorship extended beyond the initial meeting. She introduced Samantha to her network of contacts, connecting her with other experienced business leaders who shared their expertise and offered invaluable advice. One such mentor was Anya Sharma, a seasoned marketing strategist known for her innovative campaigns and her ability to connect with audiences on a deeply emotional level. Anya helped Samantha revamp her marketing strategy, focusing on authenticity and emotional storytelling, a sharp departure from the more impersonal, data-driven approach she'd used previously. Anya emphasized the importance of connecting with customers on a human level, building trust and fostering a sense of community around her brand.

Another valuable connection was made with Dr. Evelyn Reed, a renowned psychologist specializing in the psychology of entrepreneurship. Dr. Reed helped Samantha understand the emotional toll of running a business, particularly for women who often face additional pressures and societal expectations. Through therapy sessions, Samantha gained insights into her own stress management techniques and learned to prioritize self-care, recognizing that her well-being was essential to her professional success. Dr. Reed taught her techniques for managing stress and burnout, emphasizing the importance of establishing boundaries between work and personal life. This was a crucial lesson for Samantha, who had previously blurred the lines between the two, often working late into the night and neglecting her personal relationships.

These mentors didn't just offer advice; they also provided a crucial source of support and encouragement. They understood the unique challenges Samantha faced as a woman in a male-dominated industry, the pressure to constantly prove herself, the balancing act of career ambition and personal fulfillment. They listened without judgment, offering words of encouragement and validation when Samantha felt overwhelmed or discouraged. Their support helped Samantha rebuild her confidence, reminding her of her strengths and her capabilities.

The mentorship wasn't a passive process. Samantha actively sought out their guidance, preparing for meetings, engaging in thoughtful discussions, and applying their advice to her business. She wasn't afraid to ask questions, to challenge their perspectives, and to express her doubts and concerns. This active engagement was crucial to the success of the mentorship relationship. It fostered a sense of mutual respect and collaboration, transforming these relationships from transactional exchanges into genuine partnerships.

Over time, Samantha began to see the value in vulnerability. She learned that sharing her struggles and challenges with her mentors wasn't a sign of weakness, but a strength. It allowed them to offer more targeted and effective advice, and it also fostered a deeper level of connection and trust. She discovered that seeking help wasn't a sign of failure, but a sign of intelligence and self-awareness. The journey of building a successful business was a complex and multifaceted one, and accepting support didn't diminish her accomplishments; rather, it enhanced them.

One particularly insightful conversation with Isabella involved discussing the importance of delegation and trust. Samantha, in her previous attempts to maintain complete control, had micromanaged her employees, creating a stifling environment that ultimately contributed to Sarah's departure. Isabella challenged this approach, encouraging Samantha to cultivate a culture of trust and empowerment within her team. She suggested creating clear roles and responsibilities, providing adequate training and support, and giving her employees the autonomy to make decisions. This, Isabella argued, wasn't just a matter of efficiency; it was essential to fostering a positive and productive work environment where employees felt valued and respected.

The transformation wasn't immediate; it was a gradual process of learning, unlearning, and adapting. Samantha stumbled along the way, making mistakes and experiencing setbacks. But with the support of her mentors and her newly established network, she was better equipped to navigate these challenges. She learned to recognize her own limitations and to embrace the power of collaboration. She discovered that seeking help wasn't a sign of weakness but a sign of strength, a testament to her commitment to continuous growth and development.

The shift in her approach also extended to her personal life. Samantha realized that her previous neglect of her personal relationships had been a direct consequence of her obsessive focus on her career. She began to prioritize her well-being, making time for friends and family, engaging in activities that brought her joy and relaxation. This newfound balance wasn't simply a matter of adding personal time to her already overflowing schedule; it was a fundamental shift in her perspective, a recognition that her personal life was not a distraction from her professional ambitions but an integral part of her overall well-being.

The lessons she learned from her mentors transcended the realm of business. They instilled in her a deeper understanding of leadership, collaboration, and the importance of building strong, authentic relationships. She learned that true success wasn't just about achieving professional goals but about cultivating a life that was rich in meaningful connections, personal growth, and unwavering self-belief. The journey had been arduous, filled with challenges and setbacks, but the support, guidance, and wisdom she received from her mentors were invaluable, paving the way for a future where professional success and personal fulfillment could coexist harmoniously. Samantha now understood that the true measure of success lay not just in the numbers on her balance sheet, but in the richness of her life, a life lived with purpose, passion, and a deep sense of connection to herself and the world around her. The quiet hum of the city outside now held a different resonance, a symphony of accomplishment, gratitude, and hope for the future.

CHAPTER 15
Building a Strong Team

The scent of freshly brewed coffee hung in the air, a comforting aroma that mirrored the quiet confidence settling over Samantha. The office, once a place of tense energy and hushed whispers, now hummed with a renewed sense of purpose. Gone were the lingering shadows of uncertainty; in their place bloomed a vibrant energy, a testament to the careful rebuilding she had undertaken. The initial weeks had been a frantic scramble, a whirlwind of interviews, assessments, and the delicate dance of re-establishing trust and morale. But now, a solid foundation was taking shape, brick by brick, person by person.

Her new team wasn't just a collection of individuals filling roles; it was a carefully curated ensemble, each member chosen not only for their skills but also for their alignment with her vision. She had learned a valuable lesson from Isabella Rossi: a team's strength lies not just in individual brilliance but in the synergy created through shared values and a collective commitment to excellence. This wasn't simply about assembling a competent workforce; it was about cultivating a community, a cohesive unit where collaboration thrived, and every member felt valued and empowered.

One of her first priorities was to establish open communication. She instituted regular team meetings, not as formal presentations but as collaborative sessions where ideas flowed freely, challenges were openly discussed, and solutions were collaboratively crafted. She encouraged feedback, both positive and constructive, fostering a culture of transparency and mutual respect. The fear of retribution or judgment, which had been palpable during the previous regime, had been replaced by a sense of psychological safety.

Samantha knew that empowerment wasn't just about granting authority; it was about fostering ownership. She delegated tasks strategically, ensuring that each team member had the opportunity to showcase their strengths and develop new skills. She meticulously avoided micromanagement, trusting her team to deliver exceptional results. She recognized that the true measure of a leader wasn't their ability to control every aspect of the operation but their capacity to inspire and motivate their team to exceed expectations.

She implemented a system of mentorship within the team, pairing experienced employees with newer hires to foster knowledge transfer and build strong working relationships. This not only accelerated the onboarding process but also created a sense of community and shared responsibility. The experienced employees felt valued for their expertise, while the newer hires gained invaluable guidance and support. This fostered a supportive environment where everyone felt comfortable reaching out for help and sharing their challenges.

Samantha understood that a positive work environment wasn't just about the tasks at hand. It extended to fostering a sense of camaraderie and belonging. She organized teambuilding activities, both in and out of the office, to help build relationships and strengthen team cohesion. These weren't forced exercises in contrived team spirit; they were genuine opportunities for connection and fun. From casual Friday lunches to weekend hiking trips, these initiatives helped create a sense of unity and shared purpose that transcended the confines of the workplace.

She also prioritized employee well-being. She implemented a flexible work policy that respected the need for work-life balance, recognizing that happy, healthy employees are productive employees. She championed mental health awareness, encouraging open conversations about stress and burnout. She provided access to resources and support systems, ensuring that her team felt cared for not only as employees but as individuals.

One particularly poignant example was Maya, a junior developer who was struggling to meet a tight deadline. Instead of reprimanding her, Samantha sat down with Maya, listening empathetically as Maya explained the challenges she was facing. Samantha didn't offer a quick fix; she collaborated with Maya, helping her break down the project into smaller, manageable tasks, providing the support and resources she needed to succeed. This act of empathy and understanding built trust and demonstrated Samantha's genuine commitment to her team's well-being.

Another instance involved David, a senior marketing executive who had been feeling undervalued and overlooked. Samantha initiated a one-on-one meeting with David, actively listening to his concerns and acknowledging his contributions. She then collaborated with David to redefine his role, empowering him with more responsibility and autonomy. This not only revitalized David's enthusiasm but also enriched the team's strategic direction, benefiting the entire company.

The transformation wasn't immediate; it was a gradual evolution, a constant refinement of processes and relationships. There were setbacks, moments of frustration, and occasional disagreements. But Samantha's unwavering commitment to building a strong, supportive team—a team that reflected her values of collaboration, respect, and empowerment—paid off. The office atmosphere, once heavy with tension, now buzzed with creativity, energy, and a shared sense of purpose.

The change wasn't just tangible in the office; it manifested in the company's performance. Productivity soared, innovation flourished, and employee turnover plummeted. The team was no longer just a collection of individuals; it was a tightly knit unit, a force to be reckoned with. This was a testament to Samantha's leadership, her ability to inspire, motivate, and empower her team to achieve extraordinary results.

The success was not solely due to the technical proficiency of each member, but also, and perhaps more importantly, due to the powerful dynamics within the team. Samantha created an environment where constructive criticism was welcomed, ideas were nurtured, and every individual's voice held weight. This collaborative ethos extended beyond the confines of the office. Team members frequently shared their personal triumphs and challenges outside of work, creating a deep sense of camaraderie and mutual support.

The impact of this strong team extended beyond the company's bottom line. The positive work environment fostered by Samantha attracted top talent. Word spread throughout the industry about the company's supportive culture and the exceptional opportunities it provided to its employees. Samantha understood that attracting and retaining skilled employees required more than just competitive compensation; it demanded a workplace where individuals felt valued, respected, and empowered.

This realization wasn't simply a matter of good management; it was a reflection of Samantha's personal evolution. She had learned that leadership was not about dominance or control but about service, about fostering the growth and development of her team. The lessons she had absorbed from Isabella Rossi and other mentors were now deeply ingrained in her leadership philosophy. She understood that a leader's true measure lay not in their individual achievements but in the success and well-being of their team.

Samantha's journey had been one of remarkable transformation. From the depths of despair following Sarah's departure, she had emerged, stronger, wiser, and more determined than ever. She had not only rebuilt her company but had also forged a team that was not just efficient and productive but also deeply loyal and supportive. The foundation she had built wasn't just a structure of bricks and mortar, but a living, breathing organism fueled by shared purpose, mutual respect, and an unwavering belief in the power of collaboration. The quiet hum of accomplishment that she felt wasn't just a personal victory but the harmonious symphony of a team working in perfect synergy, a testament to her leadership and the power of building a truly strong and exceptional team.

CHAPTER 16
Embracing New Technologies

Samantha, ever the pragmatist, understood that clinging to outdated methods was a recipe for stagnation. Her rapid growth demanded efficiency, and efficiency, in the modern business world, meant embracing technology. This wasn't simply about adopting the latest gadgets; it was about strategically integrating technology to streamline operations, enhance customer experience, and reach a wider audience. The initial hurdle wasn't the technology itself, but the resistance to change within her own team. Many of her longtime employees, comfortable with the established routines, were apprehensive about learning new software and adapting to new workflows.

Samantha tackled this challenge with her characteristic blend of firmness and empathy. She understood the concerns, knowing that disruption could breed anxiety. Instead of imposing the changes, she organized workshops and training sessions, led by experts in the specific software and technologies they were adopting. These weren't passive lectures; they were interactive sessions designed to build confidence and demonstrate the practical benefits of the new systems. She even implemented a buddy system, pairing experienced employees with those who were struggling, fostering a collaborative learning environment. This approach proved remarkably effective, gradually easing the transition and turning skepticism into enthusiasm.

The first technology Samantha implemented was a sophisticated Customer Relationship Management (CRM) system.

This wasn't just a contact list; it was a powerful tool that tracked customer interactions, preferences, and purchasing history, providing invaluable insights into customer behavior. This allowed her team to personalize marketing campaigns, anticipate customer needs, and provide more targeted support. The results were immediate and impressive. Sales increased, customer satisfaction soared, and the overall efficiency of the customer service department improved significantly.

Next, she invested in a robust inventory management system. This automated the process of tracking stock levels, predicting demand, and optimizing ordering procedures. Gone were the days of manual spreadsheets and guesswork; the new system provided real-time data, minimizing stockouts and preventing overstocking, leading to significant cost savings. This was particularly important as her business expanded, dealing with a larger inventory and a more complex supply chain.

Samantha also recognized the power of e-commerce. While she valued the personal touch of her brick-and-mortar stores, she understood that an online presence was crucial to reach a wider market. She invested in a user-friendly website, complete with high-quality product photography, detailed descriptions, and a secure online payment gateway. This expansion wasn't without its challenges. Building a strong online presence required significant investment in website development, digital marketing, and search engine optimization. But Samantha's meticulous planning and attention to detail ensured a successful launch.

The transition to online sales also required a change in her marketing strategy. She hired a social media manager to develop engaging content, run targeted advertising campaigns, and build a strong online community. She explored various digital platforms, understanding the nuances of each channel and tailoring her approach accordingly. Her marketing efforts became more data-driven, utilizing analytics to track campaign performance and optimize spending.

Furthermore, Samantha understood the importance of data security. With the increasing reliance on digital platforms, protecting sensitive customer data became paramount. She implemented robust security measures, including encryption, firewalls, and regular security audits, ensuring the safety and privacy of customer information. This commitment to data security not only protected her customers but also built trust and enhanced her brand reputation.

The adoption of new technologies wasn't a one-time event; it was an ongoing process. Samantha fostered a culture of continuous improvement, encouraging her team to explore new tools and technologies, and to experiment with innovative solutions. Regular technology updates became a part of the company's routine, ensuring that they remained at the forefront of industry trends. She also encouraged her team to participate in industry conferences and workshops, fostering a culture of learning and development.

Beyond the practical benefits, Samantha understood that technology could also empower her employees. She equipped her team with laptops, tablets, and smartphones, enabling them to work remotely and collaborate more effectively. This flexibility improved employee satisfaction and productivity, particularly for employees with families or other commitments. She also invested in online training programs, enabling her employees to upskill and develop new competencies.

Samantha's embrace of technology wasn't solely about efficiency; it was also about creating a more engaging and personalized customer experience. She explored the use of AI-powered chatbots to provide instant customer support, and personalized email marketing campaigns to keep customers informed about new products and promotions. She also started experimenting with augmented reality (AR) technology to allow customers to virtually "try on" or visualize products before purchasing.

The integration of new technologies wasn't always smooth. There were technical glitches, software updates, and unforeseen challenges. But Samantha's unwavering commitment to innovation and her willingness to adapt ensured that these obstacles didn't derail her progress. She used these challenges as learning experiences, further refining her approach and strengthening her resilience. The overall result was a more efficient, agile, and customercentric business.

The successful integration of new technologies not only improved Samantha's business operations but also solidified her position as an innovative leader in the industry. Her willingness to embrace change, her commitment to employee development, and her strategic approach to technology adoption set a powerful example for other entrepreneurs. It demonstrated that technology, when adopted strategically and responsibly, could be a powerful catalyst for growth and success. This wasn't merely about keeping pace with technological advancements; it was about leveraging technology to create a more sustainable, efficient, and customer-centric business, a testament to Samantha's visionary leadership. This chapter in Samantha's journey was not just about technological upgrades; it was about transforming her business into a lean, mean, technologicallydriven machine, poised for even greater success. And as always, Samantha was ready for whatever the future held.

CHAPTER 17
Expanding into New Markets

The hum of the server room, once the epicenter of Samantha's technological revolution, now faded into the background as her gaze shifted outward. The domestic market, once a fertile ground for growth, was beginning to show signs of saturation. Samantha, never one to rest on her laurels, knew that true, lasting success lay in expansion. The thrill of the unknown, the challenge of conquering new territories, pulsed within her like an untamed current.

Her first foray into international markets was tentative, a carefully planned step into the vibrant tapestry of the European Union. She chose France as her initial target, drawn by its sophisticated consumer base and its reputation for appreciating quality craftsmanship, a hallmark of her company's products. But even with the meticulous research and the detailed market analysis, she quickly realized that expansion wasn't simply a matter of replicating her successful domestic strategies. It was a lesson in adaptation, a masterclass in cultural sensitivity.

The initial meetings with potential French distributors were a fascinating dance of cultural nuances. Samantha, ever the prepared businesswoman, had invested in learning basic French phrases, understanding the subtleties of French business etiquette, and researching the cultural preferences of her target audience. Even so, she was caught off guard by the emphasis on personal relationships in the French business world. In the United States, efficiency and direct communication were often prioritized. In

France, building trust and rapport, often over leisurely lunches and informal gatherings, took precedence. Samantha had initially felt that this approach was inefficient, a stark contrast to her streamlined American approach, but she quickly realized that it was an integral part of the business process in France.

Adapting meant not just changing her communication style, but also tweaking her product offerings. While her signature line resonated with the French market, she also discovered that subtle modifications – different color palettes, adjustments to packaging to align with French aesthetic preferences – were crucial for maximizing appeal. These weren't mere superficial alterations; they were strategic moves designed to resonate with the local market's cultural identity.

The launch in France proved to be a resounding success, exceeding even Samantha's ambitious projections. This initial triumph was not solely a reflection of the quality of her products, but a testament to her capacity for cultural sensitivity and adaptability. Emboldened by this victory, she shifted her attention to another continent: Asia.

Japan presented a significantly different challenge. The Japanese market was known for its discerning consumers, its meticulous attention to detail, and its deeply ingrained cultural traditions. Samantha approached the Japanese market with a blend of respect, humility, and a relentless pursuit of understanding. She immersed herself in Japanese business culture, spending considerable time studying Japanese business practices, etiquette, and communication styles. She hired local consultants to guide her through the labyrinthine complexities of the Japanese business landscape. She attended tea ceremonies, carefully observed social interactions, and sought to understand the underlying values that governed business relationships in Japan.

She learned that the concept of "ganbatte," perseverance and striving for excellence, was deeply embedded in the Japanese business ethos. She saw it reflected not just in the products but in the work ethic of the people. This understanding profoundly impacted her strategies in Japan. It wasn't enough to simply introduce her products; she had to demonstrate her commitment to quality, her dedication to excellence, and her respect for the Japanese business culture.

The marketing campaign she designed for the Japanese market differed markedly from her American campaigns. Instead of focusing on aggressive promotions and immediate sales, she opted for a more subtle, understated approach that emphasized the elegance, craftsmanship, and refined aesthetic of her products. She also partnered with reputable Japanese influencers and brands to elevate her brand's credibility and gain the trust of discerning Japanese consumers.

Expanding into Japan demanded more than just translating her marketing materials; it required a profound understanding of Japanese aesthetics and consumer psychology. She discovered that Japanese consumers valued not just the functionality of her products but their beauty, their history, and the story behind their creation. She invested heavily in communicating the story of her brand, its values, and its commitment to sustainability – all key aspects resonating deeply within Japanese culture.

Her foray into the Asian markets wasn't limited to Japan. She also strategically targeted South Korea, known for its technology-savvy and fashion-forward consumers. Here, the emphasis was on innovation, design, and social media marketing. Samantha adapted her strategies yet again, recognizing that South Korean consumers were highly responsive to social media trends and influencer marketing. She partnered with popular Korean celebrities and social media personalities to launch targeted campaigns that showcased her product's sleek design and technological innovation.

In each new market, Samantha embraced a strategy of localization, adapting her marketing messages, product design, and even her business practices to reflect the local cultural context. She recognized that a one-size-fits-all approach simply wouldn't work in the global marketplace. Each market presented unique challenges and opportunities, and her success lay in her ability to understand and respond effectively to these diverse contexts. This involved not just translating her marketing materials, but also understanding the unspoken rules and cultural nuances that governed business interactions in each region.

She established a global team, a diverse group of individuals from various backgrounds and cultures. She understood that a team with local expertise was essential for navigating the complexities of international markets. This team played a vital role in providing invaluable insights into local consumer preferences, cultural sensitivities, and regulatory requirements. They helped her identify potential pitfalls, navigate bureaucratic hurdles, and adapt her strategies to effectively reach diverse audiences.

Samantha's journey of expanding into new markets wasn't without its setbacks. There were misunderstandings, cultural mishaps, and moments of frustration. But through persistence, adaptability, and a genuine respect for the cultures she was engaging with, she consistently overcame these challenges. She learned to listen more than she spoke, to observe more than she judged, and to adapt more than she resisted.

Her international success was not solely driven by financial ambitions but by a deep-seated desire to build a global brand that celebrated diversity, embraced innovation, and championed the power of women in entrepreneurship. She understood that global expansion wasn't just about increasing profits; it was about building a community, connecting with diverse cultures, and empowering women across the globe. Her company's success served as a powerful reminder that embracing cultural differences and adapting to various contexts is not only a strategic necessity but also a rewarding path towards meaningful global impact. The world was her marketplace, and Samantha was ready to conquer it, one culturally sensitive strategy at a time.

CHAPTER 18
Product Diversification

The intoxicating scent of possibility hung heavy in the air, a fragrant blend of ambition and uncertainty. Samantha, perched on the edge of her sleek, minimalist desk, stared out at the sprawling cityscape. The initial euphoria of international expansion had begun to settle, replaced by a more measured, strategic focus. Success, she knew, wasn't a destination, but a continuous journey of adaptation and innovation. And the next leg of that journey involved a significant leap: product diversification.

Her flagship product, the revolutionary "Athena" smart home system, had been a phenomenal success. But Samantha, ever the pragmatist, understood the inherent risks of relying on a single product. Market fluctuations, technological advancements, and shifting consumer preferences could all spell disaster if she didn't diversify her offerings. This wasn't just about increasing profits; it was about building resilience, creating a more robust and sustainable business model.

The first step was thorough market research. Her team, a vibrant tapestry of talented individuals from diverse backgrounds, embarked on an extensive global study. They analyzed consumer trends, identified unmet needs, and scrutinized competitor strategies in various markets. From bustling Asian metropolises to quiet European villages, they gathered data, interviewed potential customers, and absorbed the unique cultural nuances of each region. The sheer volume of information was daunting, but

Samantha embraced the challenge, seeing it as a critical piece in her intricate puzzle of growth.

One key finding was the significant disparity in technological adoption across different regions. While the Athena system thrived in tech-savvy markets, it was too advanced, too expensive, for certain developing economies. This realization spurred the development of "Artemis," a more affordable and user-friendly smart home solution designed specifically for emerging markets. Artemis wouldn't boast the same advanced features as Athena, but it would deliver essential functionalities at a price point that was accessible and attractive to a broader consumer base. The design process was a collaborative effort, with input from engineers, designers, and marketing specialists from different cultural backgrounds. They painstakingly adapted the technology to suit local power grids, language preferences, and cultural sensitivities. The user interface was simplified, incorporating intuitive icons and voice commands in multiple languages.

The research also revealed a growing demand for environmentally friendly products. Sustainability was no longer a niche concern; it was becoming a core value for many consumers. This insight led to the creation of "Gaia," a line of eco-friendly smart home accessories designed to minimize energy consumption and reduce environmental impact. Gaia incorporated recycled materials, energyefficient components, and sustainable packaging. Its design philosophy focused on minimizing the product's carbon footprint throughout its entire lifecycle, from manufacturing to disposal.

But product diversification wasn't merely about developing new products; it was about understanding the nuances of each market and tailoring the offerings accordingly. Samantha's team conducted extensive focus groups and surveys in various regions to assess consumer preferences and tailor their marketing strategies. They learned, for example, that certain color palettes and design aesthetics resonated more strongly in some cultures than in others. Similarly, the marketing messages needed to be adapted to reflect local values and cultural sensitivities.

This meticulous approach to market research and product development paid off. Artemis quickly gained traction in emerging markets, proving that a simplified, affordable version of their core technology could still be highly successful. Gaia's eco-conscious design resonated with environmentally aware consumers globally, bolstering the company's reputation and attracting a new segment of customers. These new products not only expanded their market reach but also helped mitigate the risk associated with relying solely on the Athena system.

The diversification strategy wasn't without its challenges. Developing multiple products simultaneously demanded a significant increase in resources, both financial and human. Samantha had to carefully manage her budget, allocate resources efficiently, and ensure that the different product lines didn't cannibalize each other's sales. This involved sophisticated forecasting models and a keen understanding of the market dynamics.

She also had to build and nurture a larger, more diverse team. This required careful recruitment, thorough training, and a strong emphasis on building a collaborative and inclusive work environment. Samantha believed that diversity was not just a buzzword; it was a critical source of innovation and a key driver of success. She championed initiatives that fostered cross-cultural understanding and encouraged employees to share their unique perspectives.

Furthermore, the legal and regulatory landscape varied significantly across different regions. Samantha had to navigate complex international trade laws, intellectual property rights, and local regulations. She assembled a team of experienced international lawyers and compliance specialists to ensure that her company operated within the legal framework of each market. It was a complex and demanding task, requiring meticulous attention to detail and a deep understanding of the legal nuances of each country.

Beyond the technical and logistical challenges, Samantha faced the emotional challenge of relinquishing a degree of control. As the company expanded and diversified, she had to trust her team to manage different product lines and regional markets. This required her to delegate effectively, empower her employees, and embrace a more decentralized management style. It wasn't always easy, but she recognized that her own limitations could hinder the company's growth.

The success of Samantha's diversification strategy was a testament to her strategic vision, her ability to adapt to change, and her commitment to empowering women in technology. Her story is a powerful example of how a company can not only survive but thrive by embracing innovation, understanding market dynamics, and responding to the evolving needs of a diverse global customer base. The hum of the server room was now joined by the steady thrum of innovation, a symphony of growth and expansion echoing throughout her global enterprise. The Athena system remained a cornerstone, but it was now part of a larger, more resilient, and truly global ecosystem. The future held endless possibilities, and Samantha, armed with her vision, her resilience, and her unwavering belief in women's potential, was ready to embrace them all. The journey had only just begun.

CHAPTER 19

Investing in Research and Development

———•♡•———

The hum of the server room, once a comforting background noise, now felt like a heartbeat – the pulse of a rapidly evolving enterprise. Samantha, however, felt a different kind of pressure. The thrill of expansion had given way to a deeper, more strategic challenge: maintaining the innovative edge that had propelled Athena to global success. Her competitors, sensing her vulnerability after such rapid growth, were circling, their own ambitious projects looming on the horizon. Samantha knew she needed more than just reactive adjustments; she needed a proactive, sustained investment in research and development.

This wasn't merely about tweaking existing products or implementing minor improvements. This was a bold, ambitious commitment to future growth, a gamble on unproven technologies and potentially revolutionary concepts. It was a calculated risk, but one she was willing to take. The boardroom meetings became less about quarterly reports and more about brainstorming sessions fueled by espresso and ambitious projections. Samantha, armed with her sharp intellect and an unwavering belief in her vision, spearheaded the initiative. She presented her proposal, a meticulously crafted document detailing a significant increase in R&D funding, a plan that would shake the very foundations of the company's budget.

The initial resistance was palpable. Some board members, accustomed to more conservative strategies, expressed concerns about the financial risks. Others questioned the feasibility of some of the more audacious proposals, their skepticism echoing in the polished mahogany conference table. But Samantha, with her innate ability to inspire and persuade, patiently addressed their concerns. She presented detailed market analyses, showcasing the potential rewards far outweighing the inherent risks. She painted a vivid picture of a future where Athena wasn't just a leader in its current field, but a pioneer in entirely new markets. She spoke of groundbreaking technologies, of transformative user experiences, and of a global community empowered by Athena's innovative solutions.

Her passion was infectious. She didn't just present data; she shared a vision, a belief in the limitless possibilities of technological advancement. She showed them the potential to disrupt the industry, not just react to it. She detailed the creation of dedicated research labs, equipped with state-ofthe-art facilities and staffed by some of the brightest minds in the field – a diverse team of engineers, programmers, designers, and researchers from across the globe. She even showcased preliminary designs for new products, tantalizing glimpses of what the future held – sleek, intuitive interfaces, seamlessly integrated systems, and solutions that addressed unmet needs on a global scale.

The investment wasn't just about money; it was about talent, about fostering a culture of innovation, and about empowering the very women who would drive that innovation. Samantha implemented mentorship programs, bringing in established industry leaders to guide and inspire the younger generation of female engineers. She fostered a collaborative environment, encouraging open communication and the free exchange of ideas. She created dedicated spaces for brainstorming, innovation hubs that buzzed with energy and creativity, where fresh perspectives could flourish. She understood that true innovation didn't happen in isolation; it thrived in a supportive and collaborative ecosystem.

One of her most ambitious projects focused on developing an AI-powered system that would revolutionize personalized learning. This wasn't just about creating another educational app; it was about developing a truly adaptive platform that could tailor learning experiences to individual students, regardless of their background or learning style. The implications were profound, promising to bridge educational gaps and democratize access to high-quality education on a global scale. The team dedicated to this project worked tirelessly, conducting extensive research, developing sophisticated algorithms, and rigorously testing their prototypes. Samantha frequently visited the lab, engaging with the team, offering guidance, and celebrating their progress. She understood that progress takes time, and that nurturing creativity was just as important as meeting deadlines.

Another initiative involved the creation of a sustainable, ecofriendly data center – a bold step towards minimizing Athena's environmental footprint. This required significant investment in renewable energy sources, innovative cooling technologies, and cutting-edge energy-efficient hardware. It was a commitment to environmental responsibility that went beyond mere compliance, demonstrating Athena's dedication to building a sustainable future. This initiative not only showcased the company's environmental consciousness but also attracted investors who were increasingly focused on ESG (Environmental, Social, and Governance) factors. It became a powerful marketing tool, demonstrating that sustainable business practices and innovation could coexist and even thrive.

The transformation of Athena wasn't merely about technological advancements; it was about a shift in corporate culture. Samantha fostered an environment of continuous learning and improvement, encouraging her team to embrace failure as an opportunity for growth. Regular workshops and training sessions equipped employees with the latest skills and knowledge, while internal hackathons became breeding grounds for innovative ideas. She recognized that investing in her employees was just as important as investing in technology. Happy, engaged employees were more likely to be creative and productive.

As the months turned into years, the fruits of Samantha's investment in R&D began to ripen. New products were launched, garnering critical acclaim and market success. The AI-powered learning platform transformed educational opportunities for thousands of students globally. The sustainable data center became a model for other tech companies, showcasing the possibility of balancing innovation and environmental responsibility. Athena's reputation as a leader in innovation solidified, attracting top talent and securing strategic partnerships.

The initial skepticism within the boardroom faded, replaced by admiration and respect for Samantha's visionary leadership. Her bold gamble had paid off, not just in terms of financial returns, but also in terms of solidifying Athena's position as a global technology leader and a champion of women in the industry. The hum of the server room, once a simple sound, now resonated with the collective energy of a company pushing boundaries, transforming the world, one innovative step at a time. The future, once uncertain, now pulsed with the vibrant promise of technological advancement and empowered women leading the charge. The journey had been challenging, the investment significant, but the rewards were immeasurable – a legacy of innovation, a testament to female leadership, and a future shaped by a visionary leader's unwavering commitment to growth and progress. Samantha knew this was just the beginning; the next chapter, brimming with even more daring possibilities, awaited.

CHAPTER 20
Building a Sustainable Business

The champagne flutes felt oddly heavy in Samantha's hand. The celebratory dinner, a culmination of Athena's latest successful product launch, buzzed with the energy of accomplishment. Yet, a quiet unease lingered beneath the surface of her elation. The rapid growth, the relentless innovation – it had all come at a cost. A cost not just measured in dollars and cents, but in environmental impact and social responsibility. The realization hit her with the force of a tidal wave: Athena's future, her legacy, depended on more than just technological prowess. It depended on sustainability.

That night, as the city lights twinkled outside her hotel window, a new chapter began. It wasn't about more features, faster processors, or bigger market share; it was about building a business that thrived without compromising the planet or the people it served. The first step was a thorough internal audit. Samantha commissioned a comprehensive environmental impact assessment, scrutinizing every aspect of Athena's operations, from energy consumption in the server farms to the sourcing of materials for their products. The results were sobering. The carbon footprint was significantly larger than she'd anticipated, the waste management processes inefficient, and the reliance on nonrenewable resources alarming.

But Samantha wasn't one to shy away from daunting challenges. She assembled a dedicated sustainability team, comprised of engineers, environmental specialists, and social impact experts. Their task was monumental: to overhaul Athena's entire operational structure, transforming it into a model of environmental and social responsibility. The journey wasn't easy. There were fierce debates, pushbacks from departments resistant to change, and moments of doubt. Some team members questioned the feasibility of integrating sustainability into a fast-paced tech company; others worried about the potential financial implications. Samantha, however, remained steadfast in her vision. She knew that short-term sacrifices would lead to long-term gains, not only in terms of brand reputation and customer loyalty but also in creating a more resilient and ethical business model.

The transformation began with a commitment to renewable energy sources. Athena invested heavily in solar and wind power, gradually phasing out reliance on fossil fuels for its data centers. They implemented advanced energy management systems, optimizing energy consumption and reducing waste. The team explored innovative cooling technologies, moving away from traditional methods that consumed vast amounts of water and energy. The next phase involved a complete overhaul of their supply chain. Samantha insisted on sourcing materials from ethical and sustainable suppliers, prioritizing those committed to fair labor practices and environmental conservation. This meant meticulous vetting of suppliers, establishing transparent relationships, and a willingness to pay a premium for ethically sourced components. It wasn't the cheapest option, but it was the right one.

Simultaneously, Athena launched a robust recycling and waste reduction program. They implemented comprehensive recycling protocols, reducing landfill waste and recovering valuable materials. They invested in innovative packaging solutions, minimizing environmental impact and improving product sustainability. They even partnered with a local recycling center, offering employees training and volunteering opportunities, strengthening their connection with the community. The initiative extended beyond internal operations. Athena started partnering with environmental organizations, supporting reforestation efforts, and sponsoring educational programs focused on environmental conservation. They pledged a significant portion of their profits to charitable causes, specifically those aimed at empowering women in STEM fields and promoting environmental education in underserved communities.

The change was not just operational; it was cultural. Samantha instituted company-wide training programs, educating employees about sustainable practices and fostering a culture of environmental consciousness. She encouraged employee participation in environmental initiatives, establishing a green team to brainstorm innovative ideas and implement sustainable solutions. The company culture shifted, with employees feeling a sense of ownership and pride in Athena's commitment to sustainability.

The transformation wasn't without its hurdles. There were initial concerns about increased costs and potential impacts on profitability. Some investors questioned the long-term viability of such ambitious sustainability goals. However, Samantha's vision, coupled with the impressive data showing reduced operational costs and a significant increase in brand loyalty, proved persuasive. Customers responded enthusiastically to Athena's commitment to sustainability, rewarding the company with increased sales and strengthened brand reputation. The media lauded Athena's efforts, showcasing the company as a leader in ethical business practices. This positive media coverage, coupled with employee engagement and the resulting improved brand image, far outweighed any initial financial concerns.

Furthermore, Athena's commitment to sustainability became a significant competitive advantage. It attracted top talent, who were increasingly seeking employment with companies that aligned with their values. It fostered stronger relationships with suppliers and partners, creating a network of shared responsibility and mutual benefit. It also enhanced customer loyalty, turning ethically conscious consumers into brand advocates. Athena's story became a case study, inspiring other companies to embrace sustainable practices, proving that doing good is good for business.

Samantha found herself increasingly involved in industry forums and conferences, sharing Athena's sustainability journey and advocating for corporate social responsibility. She became a vocal champion for women in leadership, using her platform to inspire and mentor aspiring female entrepreneurs. The once-uncertain future now pulsed with purpose, driven by a potent blend of technological innovation and ethical responsibility. Athena had not just built a successful tech company; it had built a sustainable legacy, a testament to the transformative power of responsible leadership.

The hum of the server room, now powered by renewable energy, resonated with a new kind of energy – the quiet, steady hum of a business that was not only profitable but also deeply committed to the well-being of the planet and its people. Samantha looked out at the city lights, no longer feeling the weight of unease, but the gentle pressure of responsibility, a responsibility she embraced with unwavering determination. The journey had been long and challenging, but the rewards were immeasurable, extending far beyond financial success, to a legacy of sustainable innovation and empowered women leading the way. And as she raised her champagne flute, she knew this was just the beginning – a beginning built not on fleeting trends but on enduring principles of sustainability and ethical leadership. The future was bright, not just for Athena, but for a world increasingly demanding responsible business practices. The journey, she knew, was far from over, but the path was clear, and the destination, a truly sustainable and impactful future, was now within reach.

CHAPTER 21
Mentoring the Next Generation

The scent of eucalyptus hung heavy in the air as Samantha, perched on the edge of her meticulously crafted desk overlooking the sprawling city, watched the sun dip below the horizon. The cityscape, a dazzling tapestry of lights twinkling against the darkening sky, was a far cry from the star-dusted outback nights of her childhood. Yet, the quiet strength she'd honed amidst the harsh beauty of the Australian landscape remained her bedrock. This wasn't just about the empire she'd built; it was about the legacy she intended to leave. And that legacy, she realised, was inextricably linked to mentoring the next generation of female leaders.

Her office, a haven of modern elegance and understated luxury, felt strangely intimate as she welcomed Sarah, a young woman brimming with nervous energy and a business plan tucked under her arm. Sarah was the first of many; Samantha had decided to establish a formal mentorship program, a structured way to share the hard-won wisdom gleaned from years of overcoming adversity and celebrating triumphs. She'd poured over countless applications, each one a testament to the quiet ambition burning in the hearts of young women across the country. Sarah's was compelling, a blend of raw talent and unwavering determination, mirroring Samantha's own youthful fire.

"Please, have a seat," Samantha offered, her voice warm and encouraging. The years had etched lines around her eyes, but they were lines of laughter and resilience, reflecting a life lived fully and purposefully. "So, tell me about your project." Sarah launched into a detailed explanation of her app, a platform designed to connect rural communities with essential services. Samantha listened intently, her sharp mind analyzing the details, identifying potential pitfalls, and recognizing the brilliance of the core concept. This wasn't simply about evaluating a business plan; it was about nurturing a dream, fostering confidence, and guiding a fledgling entrepreneur through the intricate maze of the business world.

Samantha's approach was less about dispensing ready-made answers and more about asking probing questions, prompting self-reflection, and helping Sarah uncover her own solutions. "What are your biggest concerns?" she inquired, her gaze piercing yet supportive.

Sarah hesitated, her initial enthusiasm tempered by a wave of self-doubt. "Funding," she confessed, her voice barely a whisper. "Securing enough funding to get the app off the ground is proving incredibly challenging."

Samantha nodded sympathetically, recognizing the familiar pang of frustration. She recounted her own struggles with securing initial funding, the countless rejections, and the unwavering belief in her vision that propelled her forward. "It's a tough battle, Sarah," she acknowledged, "but don't let it derail you. Rejection is simply redirection. It's about learning from each setback, refining your pitch, and persistently pursuing your goal."

Over the next few months, Samantha guided Sarah through every stage of the process. They discussed everything from securing funding to developing a marketing strategy, from building a strong team to navigating legal and regulatory hurdles. Samantha introduced Sarah to her network of trusted advisors, seasoned professionals who readily offered their expertise and support. She wasn't just sharing her knowledge; she was building a bridge, connecting Sarah to a network of support that would propel her forward.

The mentorship was more than just business advice; it was about fostering confidence and nurturing self-belief. Samantha saw in Sarah a reflection of her younger self – the raw talent, the burning ambition, and the hesitant steps towards a audacious dream. She shared her experiences, both triumphs and failures, emphasizing the importance of resilience and the power of believing in oneself, even when faced with overwhelming odds.

Their sessions weren't confined to the sterile environment of Samantha's office. Sometimes they met over coffee, amidst the bustling energy of a city café, other times amidst the tranquil beauty of a coastal walk, the rhythmic crash of waves providing a soothing backdrop to their discussions. These informal encounters allowed for a deeper connection, a more candid sharing of experiences and vulnerabilities.

Beyond Sarah, Samantha mentored countless other women, each with their unique aspirations and challenges. She established workshops, seminars, and online forums, creating a vibrant community of support and collaboration. Her mentorship wasn't about creating clones of herself; it was about empowering each individual to find their own path to success, to build their own unique brand, and to discover their own leadership style.

Samantha's mentorship went beyond simply imparting business skills. She emphasized the importance of ethical leadership, sustainable practices, and social responsibility. She encouraged her mentees to prioritize work-life balance, to value their well-being, and to never compromise their values in pursuit of success. She challenged them to think beyond profit and to consider the broader impact of their businesses on society.

One mentee, Anya, initially struggled with the notion of balancing her entrepreneurial aspirations with her desire to start a family. Samantha shared her own experience, the sacrifices she made, and the importance of finding support and building a strong support system. She emphasized the importance of setting boundaries, prioritizing self-care, and delegating tasks when necessary. Anya, armed with Samantha's insights and encouragement, successfully launched her eco-friendly fashion label while also embracing motherhood.

Another mentee, Chloe, initially lacked confidence in her abilities. Samantha spent countless hours working with Chloe, patiently building her self-esteem, identifying her strengths, and helping her overcome her self-doubt. Chloe, empowered by Samantha's belief in her, went on to create a groundbreaking app for sustainable agriculture, a testament to the transformative power of mentorship.

These success stories weren't just personal victories for her mentees; they were a testament to Samantha's unwavering commitment to empowering the next generation of female leaders. Her legacy extended beyond the business empire she'd painstakingly built; it was about the ripple effect of her influence, the countless women she had empowered to pursue their dreams, and the positive impact they were having on the world. The city lights twinkling below weren't merely a symbol of her success; they were a beacon of hope, illuminating the path for generations to come. And as Samantha watched the stars emerge, she knew that her true legacy was not in the buildings she built, but in the women she had helped to build themselves.

CHAPTER 22
The Empowerment Hub

The quiet hum of the city faded as Samantha leaned back in her chair, a steaming mug of chamomile tea warming her hands. The panoramic view, usually a source of quiet pride, felt strangely insignificant tonight. Her gaze drifted beyond the glittering skyline, settling on the far-off constellation of lights that marked the outskirts of the city – lights that represented not just homes, but lives touched, communities strengthened, dreams ignited. Her business empire, impressive as it was, felt less significant than the quiet, profound changes happening on a grassroots level, changes she was actively contributing to.

Her philanthropic work, initially a small trickle, had grown into a powerful river, shaping the landscape of her community and beyond. It started subtly, with small donations to local women's shelters, sponsoring educational programs for underprivileged girls, and funding micro-loan initiatives for budding female entrepreneurs. But her vision had expanded, driven by the unwavering belief that true success was measured not solely by financial gains but by the positive impact one made on the lives of others.

One of her most ambitious projects was the "Empowerment Hub," a state-of-the-art center designed to provide comprehensive support to women facing economic hardship. It housed vocational training facilities, childcare services, and mentorship programs, offering a holistic approach to empowerment. The hub buzzed with activity – the rhythmic tap-tap-tap of sewing machines, the animated chatter of women engaged in coding workshops, the quiet concentration of others attending business management seminars. Samantha often visited, not as a benefactor observing from afar, but as a participant, engaging with the women, sharing stories, offering encouragement, and learning from their resilience.

The impact was palpable. Stories of transformation unfolded daily. There was Fatima, a single mother who, through the Hub's vocational training program, learned to design and create exquisite textiles, eventually establishing her own small business and providing a stable life for her children. Then there was Anya, a young woman who overcame years of self-doubt to pursue her passion for technology, landing a well-paying job after completing the Hub's coding program. These weren't just statistics; they were living testaments to the power of opportunity and support.

Beyond the Empowerment Hub, Samantha's philanthropic arm extended into various other initiatives. She established scholarships for young women pursuing STEM fields, a crucial step in bridging the gender gap in science and technology. She partnered with environmental organizations to support sustainable development projects in rural communities, recognizing the critical link between economic opportunity and environmental protection. She funded research into women's health, believing that access to quality healthcare was a fundamental right, not a privilege. Each project, meticulously researched and implemented, reflected her deep-seated commitment to creating a more equitable and sustainable world.

Her giving wasn't limited to financial contributions. She invested her time, her expertise, and her influence, mentoring countless women, both personally and through the Hub's mentorship programs. She understood the power of human connection, the profound impact of a listening ear, and the transformative potential of a belief in one's ability to succeed.

She encouraged her mentees to not only build their own empires but to give back to their communities, fostering a culture of generosity and social responsibility that rippled outwards.

The scale of her philanthropy was remarkable, but what truly set it apart was the personal touch, the genuine care she showed for the individuals she was helping. It wasn't about writing a check and moving on; it was about building relationships, understanding their struggles, and celebrating their triumphs. She attended graduation ceremonies, celebrated entrepreneurial successes, and offered unwavering support during times of adversity. Her presence, her genuine engagement, served as a constant reminder that they were not forgotten, that they were valued, and that their contributions mattered.

One particular project held a special place in Samantha's heart – a community garden project in a low-income neighborhood. The garden wasn't just about providing fresh produce; it was a catalyst for community building, fostering connections between neighbors, creating a sense of shared purpose, and empowering residents to take ownership of their surroundings. The vibrant colors of the garden, the laughter of children playing amidst the rows of vegetables, the sense of collective achievement – it was a tangible expression of the positive impact she sought to create.

Samantha realized that her legacy wouldn't be solely defined by the size of her bank account or the impressive list of awards she'd received. It would be defined by the lives she'd touched, the dreams she'd helped realize, and the ripple effect of empowerment that continued to expand long after she was gone. The Empowerment Hub, the scholarships, the community garden – these weren't just projects; they were tangible expressions of her values, her vision for a more just and equitable world. They were the bricks and mortar of a legacy built not on steel and concrete but on human connection, resilience, and the unwavering belief in the power of collective action.

The sun rose, casting a golden glow on the city, painting the sky in hues of optimism and hope. Samantha looked out at the sprawling metropolis, no longer seeing just lights, but a tapestry of lives woven together, lives touched by kindness, opportunity, and the unwavering belief in human potential. Her empire, indeed, extended far beyond the skyscrapers and boardrooms. It extended to the hearts and minds of the countless women she'd empowered, their stories becoming chapters in her own enduring legacy. And as she sipped her tea, she felt a deep sense of contentment, a quiet satisfaction that transcended mere financial success. This was her true wealth, her lasting legacy – a legacy built on giving back, on empowering others, and on the quiet, profound power of human connection. It was a legacy she would continue to nurture, a legacy that would continue to blossom long after she was gone, leaving its mark on generations to come. And in the quiet stillness of the morning, she knew, with unwavering certainty, that this was a legacy worth building. The city below was not just a symbol of her own achievement, but a testament to the collective power of dreams realized, a symphony of hope orchestrated by countless individuals working together to build a brighter future – a future she had had a hand in shaping. This was the true measure of her success, far surpassing any financial milestone. This was a legacy built on the foundation of compassion, empowerment, and an unwavering belief in the potential of every human being. And as she looked towards the future, she felt a surge of optimism and a renewed determination to continue her work, to continue inspiring, and to continue giving back to the community that had given her so much. The work was far from over, but the journey was incredibly rewarding, and she felt immensely grateful for the opportunity to make a difference.

CHAPTER 23
Navigating Complex Relationships

The city hummed a different tune that morning. The optimistic sunrise felt less vibrant, the energy less buoyant. Samantha's usual pre-dawn clarity was clouded by a nagging unease. It stemmed not from the pressures of her empire, but from the delicate, fraying threads of her personal relationships. The demands of her business, while fulfilling, had inadvertently created a chasm between her and those closest to her.

Her husband, Daniel, a supportive and loving partner, felt increasingly sidelined. His own career, once a vibrant source of shared pride, had taken a backseat to Samantha's meteoric rise. He'd expressed his concerns subtly at first – a fleeting comment about missed anniversaries, a slightly strained smile during a late-night phone call. But lately, the silences had become deafening, the unspoken resentments accumulating like a slow, insidious poison. He wasn't angry, not exactly. More...disappointed. And that hurt Samantha more than any outright confrontation.

She understood his perspective, even empathized with it. The constant travel, the never-ending meetings, the unrelenting pressure – it had all taken its toll. She'd sacrificed time with him, with their friends, even with herself, in pursuit of her vision. The guilt gnawed at her, a persistent undercurrent beneath the surface of her accomplishments.

Her relationship with her sister, Emily, was equally strained. Emily, a talented artist with a more bohemian lifestyle, often felt overshadowed by Samantha's success. While she outwardly celebrated Samantha's achievements, a simmering resentment lurked beneath. Emily felt Samantha was too focused on her work, losing touch with the simple joys of life – the intimate conversations, the shared laughter, the sisterly bond that had once been their bedrock. The distance was palpable during their infrequent phone calls, their once effortless conversations now stilted and strained.

Samantha knew that the key to mending these fractured relationships wasn't grand gestures or expensive apologies, but rather consistent, heartfelt effort. It meant scheduling time, truly scheduling it, for her loved ones – not just squeezing in fleeting moments between meetings. It meant listening, truly listening, to their concerns, validating their feelings without resorting to defensive justifications. It meant consciously choosing to put down her phone, silence the incessant notifications, and simply be present.

She started small. She cancelled a planned business trip, opting instead for a weekend getaway with Daniel. They rented a cozy cabin in the mountains, disconnecting from the digital world and reconnecting with each other. It wasn't easy. The old patterns, the ingrained habits, were hard to break. Samantha found herself constantly checking her emails, her mind still buzzing with business concerns. But Daniel, to his credit, was patient, understanding. He gently guided her back to the present, reminding her to focus on the quiet moments, the shared laughter, the simple joy of being together. They talked, truly talked, about their dreams, their fears, their unspoken resentments. The conversation was difficult, raw, emotionally charged, but it was also healing, cathartic.

With Emily, the reconciliation was more gradual, more nuanced. Samantha initiated a weekly phone call, specifically setting aside an hour to connect, free from distractions. She listened intently as Emily talked about her art, her frustrations, her hopes. She asked questions, genuinely interested in her sister's life, not just making polite inquiries. They reconnected over shared memories, rediscovering the deep bond that had been temporarily obscured by distance and competing priorities. Samantha even made a point of visiting Emily's studio, offering genuine appreciation for her work, her unique perspective, her talent.

The process wasn't without its setbacks. There were still moments of frustration, of miscommunication, of lingering resentment. But Samantha persevered, driven by a profound understanding that her legacy extended far beyond her business empire. It encompassed the quality of her relationships, the depth of her connections, the love she shared with those closest to her.

She began delegating more effectively, learning to trust her team, to empower them to take on more responsibility. This freed up her time, allowing her to be more present in her personal life. She also consciously incorporated mindfulness practices into her routine, finding solace in meditation and yoga, helping her manage stress and center herself.

The change wasn't overnight. It was a gradual, ongoing process, requiring constant effort, self-reflection, and a willingness to adapt. But as the months passed, the chasm between her business and personal life began to narrow. The strained silences were replaced with genuine conversations, the unspoken resentments with open communication, the distance with intimacy.

One evening, as she sat with Daniel, sharing a quiet dinner, she realized the profound shift that had taken place. The weight of her responsibilities still existed, but it no longer felt crushing. It felt manageable, sustainable. She'd found a rhythm, a balance, a way to honor both her ambitions and her relationships. She saw the love in Daniel's eyes, felt the warmth of his touch, and experienced a sense of peace she hadn't known before. The legacy she was building was no longer solely defined by her business success; it was defined by the strength of her relationships, the richness of her connections, the love she shared with the people who mattered most.

Her relationship with Emily also blossomed. They started painting together, their canvases filled with laughter and shared memories. Samantha realized that the success she'd achieved was not just her own, but a reflection of the support system she'd cultivated. Her success was intertwined with the love and understanding she'd found in her personal life.

Samantha's journey wasn't about achieving a perfect balance – perfection is an illusion, unattainable. It was about consciously striving for a harmonious existence, where her professional aspirations and personal relationships could coexist and thrive. It was about understanding that true leadership extended beyond boardrooms and spreadsheets, encompassing empathy, compassion, and the unwavering commitment to nurturing the relationships that gave her life meaning.

As she looked out at the city lights once more, they no longer represented just a symbol of her business empire but a reflection of her well-rounded life – a life built on the foundation of hard work, but also on love, forgiveness, and the enduring strength of human connection. The legacy she was building extended far beyond her professional achievements; it encompassed the love she shared with her family and friends, the connections she nurtured, and the profound impact she had on the lives of those around her. It was a testament to the fact that true success is not just about reaching the top, but about making the journey meaningful, fulfilling, and deeply human. The city's symphony of lights now echoed not just her professional success but also the quiet, profound harmony she had finally found in her life –

a legacy built on love, balance, and the unwavering strength of human connection. And as she drifted off to sleep, she knew that this was a legacy truly worth cherishing.

CHAPTER 24

Celebrating Milestones and Achievements

The champagne bubbles tickled Samantha's nose, a tiny, celebratory rebellion against the quiet gravity of the moment. The penthouse suite, usually a whirlwind of activity, was hushed, bathed in the soft glow of the city lights twinkling far below. Tonight, it was just her, a half-empty flute, and the panoramic view of her empire. Tonight, she celebrated.

It wasn't a lavish gala, no throngs of well-wishers or flashing cameras. This celebration was intimate, a quiet acknowledgment of a journey that had been both exhilarating and exhausting. She raised her glass, not to the skyscrapers that clawed at the night sky, but to the quiet victories, the hard-fought battles, and the unexpected grace that had shaped her life.

The first milestone that swam into her memory was the small, cramped office she'd rented years ago, a space barely large enough for a desk and a chair. It had been a haven of chaotic energy, fuelled by instant coffee and unwavering determination. The air had been thick with the scent of ambition, a heady perfume she still remembered vividly. From that tiny room, she'd built something magnificent, something that reflected not only her business acumen but her unwavering belief in herself.

She thought of the early struggles, the sleepless nights spent poring over spreadsheets and strategizing, the countless rejections that had tested her resilience. Those moments, once filled with despair, now felt like badges of honor, testaments to her perseverance. Each rejection, each setback, had only served to strengthen her resolve, honing her skills and sharpening her focus. She'd learned to embrace failure as a stepping stone, not a stumbling block, transforming setbacks into opportunities for growth. This realization, she now understood, was one of the most significant milestones of her journey.

Then there was the acquisition of her first major client – a moment that had felt like a validation of all her hard work and sacrifices. The initial contract, signed with a trembling hand, was framed and hung in her office, a constant reminder of the pivotal moment that had propelled her forward. It was a symbol of the trust she'd earned, a validation of her capabilities, and a testament to her growing reputation in the industry. The memories of the celebrations following that breakthrough – the shared laughter, the triumphant cheers – warmed her heart even now.

The subsequent successes flowed like a river, each one building upon the last. She recalled the launch of her first innovative product, a product born from countless hours of research and development, a product that had disrupted the market and redefined industry standards. The overwhelming response, the positive reviews, the surge in sales – it had all felt surreal, a dream come true. But it was a dream she had worked tirelessly to achieve.

But beyond the financial triumphs, Samantha recognized another profound milestone: the development of her leadership style. She'd learned that true leadership wasn't about wielding power but about empowering others. It was about fostering collaboration, creating a supportive environment, and inspiring those around her to reach their full potential. She remembered the countless hours she'd spent mentoring younger colleagues, sharing her knowledge and experience, guiding them through their own challenges. The pride she felt in their accomplishments mirrored the pride she felt in her own.

This recognition of her strengths, not just her business acumen, but her leadership qualities, was a pivotal moment in her self-discovery. She learned to listen more, to delegate effectively, and to trust her team's expertise. This shift wasn't just good for business; it created a more fulfilling and balanced work environment. It was a testament to her evolution as a leader and as a person.

Her celebration tonight wasn't merely about the accumulation of wealth or the expansion of her business empire. It was about the profound personal growth she'd experienced throughout her journey. It was about acknowledging the sacrifices she'd made, the challenges she'd overcome, and the unwavering support she'd received from family and friends.

She thought of her parents, their unwavering belief in her providing a bedrock of support during the toughest times. She thought of her close-knit circle of friends, who had celebrated her successes and offered solace during her moments of doubt. Their unwavering support had been her constant anchor, reminding her of the importance of human connection amidst the relentless pursuit of her goals.

Samantha understood that success was not a solitary pursuit; it was a collective effort, a symphony of collaboration and shared experience. The success she celebrated tonight belonged not only to her but to all those who had contributed to her journey.

As the city lights shimmered outside, she realized that the true legacy she was building wasn't just about the business she'd created but about the people she'd touched along the way. She'd helped countless individuals achieve their own goals, provided opportunities for growth, and created a culture of empowerment. That, she realized, was the most enduring legacy of all.

The quiet moments of reflection, the acknowledgment of her personal growth and the relationships she'd nurtured – these were the unsung heroes of her success story, the quiet milestones that held far more value than any financial achievement.

The champagne was gone now, the city lights seemed to dim slightly as dawn approached. But Samantha felt a different kind of glow, an inner radiance emanating from the deep satisfaction of a journey well-travelled, a journey marked not just by milestones achieved, but by the lessons learned and the relationships fostered. It was a feeling of contentment, a quiet pride in the life she'd built, not just the empire, but the balanced, fulfilling existence she had created for herself.

Her legacy, she realized, was not just a testament to ambition and hard work, but a powerful narrative about resilience, growth, and the unwavering importance of human connection. It was a story she'd continue to write, each chapter enriched by the lessons learned, the challenges overcome, and the unwavering support of those closest to her. The city lights held a new meaning now, a reflection not just of her business empire, but of the rich tapestry of her life, a life she had built with intention, passion, and an unwavering commitment to her values. And as the first rays of sun touched the horizon, she knew that the most important celebration lay not in the past, but in the bright promise of the future. The future she was ready to embrace, armed with wisdom, gratitude, and an unwavering belief in herself and her capacity to achieve even greater things.

This was not an ending, but a beginning, a new chapter in her life's extraordinary story. A story she was determined to continue writing, one filled with even more incredible milestones, unwavering friendships, and a legacy of inspiration that would extend far beyond her own lifetime. The journey, she knew, was far from over, and she was ready to embrace whatever challenges lay ahead with the same resilience, grace, and unwavering belief in herself that had brought her to this moment of profound contentment and quiet celebration.

105

CHAPTER 25

Embracing the Future

The sunrise painted the cityscape in hues of rose and gold, a breathtaking backdrop to the quiet contemplation that filled Samantha's penthouse. The celebratory champagne had long since been replaced by a steaming cup of herbal tea, its calming aroma a comforting counterpoint to the thrill of the previous night. The past, with its triumphs and tribulations, felt both distant and intimately close, a tapestry woven with threads of hard work, sacrifice, and unexpected joy. But the dawn brought with it a sharp focus on the future, a future she was not only ready for, but actively shaping.

Her legacy, she mused, wasn't just about the buildings she'd built, the companies she'd founded, or the financial success she'd achieved. It was about the ripple effect, the inspiration she'd unknowingly provided to countless women who saw in her journey a reflection of their own aspirations. It was about the team she had nurtured, the lives she had touched, and the values she had tirelessly championed. This realization filled her with a profound sense of purpose, a driving force that propelled her forward, not with ambition alone, but with a deep sense of responsibility.

The next chapter, she knew, wouldn't be about conquering new peaks alone. It was about building bridges, fostering collaboration, and empowering the next generation of leaders. This meant investing heavily in mentorship programs, fostering a culture of inclusivity within her organization, and actively seeking out and supporting women-led ventures. She envisioned a future where her company wasn't just a successful enterprise, but a catalyst for positive change, a beacon of opportunity for women across various industries.

Her approach to the future was not based on impulsive decisions or fleeting trends, but on a carefully crafted strategy rooted in continuous learning and adaptation. She planned to establish a robust research and development department focused on sustainable and innovative solutions, anticipating future market demands and aligning her business with evolving societal needs. She saw the potential for her company to be at the forefront of technological advancements, pioneering new approaches in renewable energy, sustainable manufacturing, and ethical sourcing.

This wasn't simply about staying ahead of the curve; it was about responsible growth, mindful expansion, and a commitment to making a lasting positive impact on the world. She planned to integrate principles of environmental stewardship into every facet of her business, from reducing carbon emissions to promoting ethical labor practices. She envisioned a future where her company was not just financially successful, but also environmentally and socially responsible, a model for others to emulate.

Beyond the business realm, Samantha recognized the importance of personal growth and self-care in sustaining her vision for the future. She committed to allocating more time for activities that nurtured her creativity, her physical well-being, and her spiritual growth. This included dedicated time for meditation, yoga, and spending time in nature, activities that helped her maintain clarity, focus, and a sense of inner peace. She understood that her capacity to lead effectively was intrinsically linked to her personal wellbeing, and she made a conscious effort to prioritize both.

She also recognized the importance of building and maintaining strong relationships, both personal and professional. The support network she had cultivated over the years had been instrumental to her success, and she intended to cherish and nurture those connections. She planned to spend more quality time with her family and friends, recognizing that genuine human connection was the bedrock of her happiness and success. She believed in the power of community, and she envisioned a future where her professional and personal spheres enriched each other, creating a harmonious and fulfilling life.

Samantha's approach to the future wasn't about conquering fear, but about embracing uncertainty with courage and resilience. She knew that challenges were inevitable, and that setbacks were opportunities for growth and learning. She planned to approach obstacles with a mindset of adaptability and resourcefulness, viewing them as puzzles to be solved rather than insurmountable barriers. Her past experiences had taught her the importance of perseverance, and she was prepared to face whatever came her way with unwavering determination.

Her strategy for navigating the future also included a conscious effort to delegate responsibilities and empower her team. She recognized the immense talent within her organization and intended to foster a culture of collaboration, trust, and mutual respect. She believed in empowering her employees to take ownership of their work, to make decisions independently, and to contribute their unique skills and perspectives to the collective success of the company. She saw this not as relinquishing control, but as a means of amplifying the organization's potential.

Furthermore, Samantha's vision for the future extended beyond the confines of her own company. She planned to actively participate in initiatives that promoted women's empowerment and entrepreneurship, sharing her knowledge and experience to help other women achieve their dreams.

She envisioned a future where more women held leadership positions in various sectors, and she was committed to playing a role in making that vision a reality. This commitment stemmed from a deep belief in the importance of diversity and inclusion, recognizing the richness and strength that diverse perspectives brought to any endeavor.

This wasn't a mere business plan; it was a blueprint for a life lived with intention, purpose, and a profound sense of gratitude. It was a future built on a foundation of resilience, learned wisdom, and the unwavering belief in her ability to make a difference. Samantha wasn't just planning her future; she was creating it, one thoughtful decision, one strategic move, one act of kindness at a time. The sun climbed higher, illuminating the cityscape with its brilliance, a fitting metaphor for the bright and hopeful future Samantha was confidently embracing. Her journey, she knew, was far from over, but the path ahead was clear, illuminated by the lessons learned and the unwavering belief in herself and her capacity to create a truly impactful and lasting legacy. The champagne had been celebratory, but this new dawn held a promise far deeper and more profound – the promise of a future built on purpose, resilience, and an enduring commitment to making a positive impact on the world. And as she sipped her tea, looking out at the city awakening around her, Samantha felt a profound sense of peace, a quiet confidence in the journey that lay ahead. This was not just the next chapter; it was the unfolding of a life lived authentically, purposefully, and with unwavering grace.

CHAPTER 26
The Impact of Samantha's Success

Samantha's success reverberated far beyond the confines of her own business empire. It wasn't merely about the impressive figures on her balance sheet or the accolades lining her shelves; it was about the ripple effect her journey created, a seismic shift in the Australian business landscape, particularly for women. Her story became a beacon, illuminating a path previously shrouded in shadow for countless aspiring female entrepreneurs.

The most immediate impact was felt within the Australian business community. Samantha's unwavering determination and resilience, documented extensively in media coverage and business publications, resonated deeply with other women. Her success shattered the glass ceiling, not with a single, resounding crack, but with a series of carefully orchestrated blows, each one demonstrating the power of perseverance and strategic thinking. Suddenly, the narrative shifted. It wasn't just about male-dominated industries; it was about women carving their own niches, establishing themselves as leaders, and demanding their rightful place at the table.

Her influence extended beyond individual inspiration. Samantha's achievements spurred policy changes aimed at fostering female entrepreneurship. Government initiatives emerged, mirroring her entrepreneurial spirit, providing funding opportunities, mentorship programs, and access to resources specifically designed to empower women in business. These were not mere symbolic gestures; they were concrete steps taken in response to a demonstrable need, a need Samantha had, through her own remarkable journey, brought to the forefront of public consciousness.

Moreover, her philanthropic endeavors played a significant role in shaping the landscape of Australian business. Samantha's commitment to giving back to her community wasn't a mere afterthought; it was an integral part of her business philosophy. A substantial portion of her profits were channeled into initiatives supporting women's education, skill development, and access to financial resources. She established scholarships, funded mentorship programs, and created networking opportunities, nurturing a new generation of female leaders. This investment in human capital created a virtuous cycle, fostering growth not just within her own company, but across the wider business ecosystem.

The impact of her philanthropy was far-reaching. It provided critical support to women from disadvantaged backgrounds, providing them with the tools and resources they needed to break the cycle of poverty and pursue their dreams. Her commitment transcended mere financial assistance; she actively championed these women, offering guidance, mentorship, and unwavering support. She actively sought out and nurtured talent, ensuring that every opportunity was seized. This commitment to fostering talent ensured a positive feedback loop, allowing the benefits of her philanthropic actions to continue multiplying. Samantha's actions directly influenced the lives of countless women and proved the profound influence that one individual could have on an entire community.

Her impact also extended beyond immediate financial support. Samantha became a role model, embodying the qualities of resilience, determination, and unwavering belief in oneself. Her story transcended the purely professional; it became a narrative of personal empowerment, inspiring women from all walks of life to pursue their own ambitions, irrespective of the obstacles in their path. Her success wasn't solely measured in monetary terms; it was about shattering societal expectations, demonstrating the potential within each individual, and inspiring others to pursue their own dreams. Her narrative resonated with a generation of women who felt empowered to step out of their comfort zones, pursue ambitious ventures, and defy traditional roles.

Samantha's legacy wasn't confined to Australia. Her story, disseminated through various media platforms, inspired women globally. International conferences invited her to share her experiences, her insights translated into different languages, her journey resonating across cultural boundaries. Her success became a testament to the universality of the female entrepreneurial spirit, a symbol of hope and empowerment for women worldwide. Her story served as a powerful reminder that success is attainable, regardless of background or circumstances.

This international recognition further solidified her influence. Her story became a case study in business schools, analyzed and dissected as a model of entrepreneurial success, highlighting her strategic decision-making, risktaking abilities and her unwavering commitment to ethical practices. The impact rippled outwards, influencing both academic thought and industry practice, enriching the curriculum and shaping the next generation of business leaders, encouraging innovative approaches and responsible practices. Her impact transcended the Australian business landscape, serving as a global example of entrepreneurial excellence.

Her enduring influence continued through various initiatives. She established a mentorship program, directly engaging with aspiring entrepreneurs, offering guidance and support based on her own experiences. She acted as a sounding board, offering advice, providing connections and sharing invaluable insights, fostering a network of support for other women. She understood the value of community and collaboration and actively worked to create a supportive environment where women could thrive. She wasn't just a successful businesswoman; she became a mentor, a guide, a trusted confidante, a facilitator of success for countless others.

Samantha's commitment to ongoing engagement in industry discussions, conferences and public forums solidified her role as a thought leader. She used her platform to advocate for policy changes, to address persistent challenges faced by women in business, and to champion initiatives promoting gender equality. Her voice became a powerful instrument for change, influencing conversations, shaping policies, and promoting inclusivity within the business world. She transformed from a successful entrepreneur into an influential advocate, actively shaping the landscape for future generations of female entrepreneurs.

The impact of her story on a new generation of female entrepreneurs is perhaps her most significant legacy. Her journey became a powerful narrative, shared and re-shared, inspiring countless young women to pursue their own entrepreneurial ambitions. Her success proved that it was possible to defy expectations, to overcome obstacles, to build a successful business on one's own terms. She showed that it was possible to balance ambition with integrity, to achieve professional success while maintaining personal values. Her story resonated deeply, giving hope, encouragement, and the vital belief that success was attainable.

Samantha became a symbol of female empowerment, transcending the purely commercial aspect of her success.

Her story became a powerful narrative of resilience, tenacity and unwavering self-belief, demonstrating the potential of every woman. Her journey provided inspiration, demonstrating that barriers can be broken, challenges overcome and aspirations realised. Her success became a beacon of hope, encouraging women to pursue their ambitions regardless of societal expectations. Her narrative became a powerful testament to the strength, determination, and potential of women.

Looking back on her journey, Samantha's story isn't just about building a successful business; it's about forging a path, breaking down barriers, and inspiring others to do the same. Her resilience, her determination, her unwavering belief in herself – these are the qualities that fueled her success and continue to inspire generations to come. Her journey is a testament to the power of human potential, a reminder that with hard work, dedication, and a unwavering belief in oneself, even the most audacious dreams can be realized. Samantha's story is a celebration of the female spirit, a resounding testament to the potential of every woman to achieve greatness, a legacy that will continue to inspire and empower for decades to come.

CHAPTER 27
Samantha's Enduring Influence

Even after stepping down from the daily grind of running her empire, Samantha's influence only intensified. Retirement, for her, wasn't about slowing down; it was about strategically shifting gears. She saw a vast untapped potential in nurturing the next generation of female entrepreneurs, a vision fueled by her own experiences and the countless women who had reached out to her over the years, inspired by her story. This led to the creation of the "Samantha Reed Mentorship Program," a carefully curated initiative designed to provide aspiring female business leaders with the guidance, resources, and support they needed to navigate the oftenchallenging terrain of the Australian business world.

The program wasn't a generic, one-size-fits-all approach. Samantha understood the unique challenges faced by women in business – the subtle biases, the uphill battles against ingrained societal expectations, the struggle for equal footing in a male-dominated world. She designed the program to address these issues head-on, offering personalized mentorship, workshops on overcoming systemic obstacles, and networking opportunities with established female leaders across various industries. The program's success was immediate and resounding. Within its first year, hundreds of women applied, vying for a coveted spot in the program. Samantha, with her characteristic dedication and insightful guidance, personally reviewed each application, ensuring that the selected participants were not just driven and ambitious but also possessed the resilience and integrity she valued so highly.

The mentorship program wasn't merely about imparting business acumen; it was about fostering a supportive community. Samantha cultivated a sisterhood amongst the participants, encouraging collaboration, mutual support, and the sharing of experiences, both triumphs and setbacks. Regular workshops focused on everything from financial planning and strategic marketing to negotiation tactics and stress management—all crucial aspects that Samantha had learned throughout her journey. But perhaps the most valuable aspect was the opportunity to learn directly from Samantha herself. Her candid discussions, sharing both her successes and her failures, resonated deeply with the participants, offering invaluable lessons beyond textbooks and business plans. She emphasized the importance of selfbelief, the necessity of perseverance, and the power of embracing failure as a learning opportunity.

Beyond the mentorship program, Samantha channeled her energy into philanthropic endeavors, believing that giving back was an integral part of her legacy. She established the "Samantha Reed Foundation," dedicated to supporting women-led social enterprises and providing educational opportunities for girls in underprivileged communities. The Foundation's focus was on empowering women at every stage of life, from providing scholarships for young girls aspiring to pursue higher education to funding innovative social ventures that addressed issues like poverty, inequality, and lack of access to healthcare. Samantha's commitment to the Foundation wasn't simply a financial one; she actively participated in its operations, traveling to remote communities to meet the beneficiaries and personally oversee the impact of the Foundation's projects.

Her involvement in industry discussions further solidified her enduring influence. Samantha remained a sought-after speaker at conferences and industry events, sharing her insights on leadership, innovation, and the importance of fostering a more inclusive and equitable business environment. Her presentations weren't dry lectures filled with jargon; they were compelling narratives interwoven with personal anecdotes, illustrating her points with relatable experiences and empowering stories. She captivated her audiences, inspiring them with her unwavering optimism and her unwavering belief in the potential of women to transform the world.

Her speeches weren't just about her own success; they were about advocating for change, for creating a level playing field where women could thrive. She challenged the status quo, openly addressing the systemic inequalities and biases that still permeated the Australian business landscape. She wasn't afraid to speak truth to power, using her platform to advocate for policies that supported women's economic empowerment and called for greater representation of women in leadership roles.

Samantha's legacy extended beyond boardrooms and conference halls. Her story became a case study in business schools, inspiring aspiring entrepreneurs to pursue their dreams with unwavering determination. Books and articles were written about her, chronicling her remarkable journey and highlighting the impact of her entrepreneurial spirit and her commitment to social justice. Her life story became a testament to the transformative power of female leadership, demonstrating that success could be defined not only by financial achievements but also by the positive impact one could have on society.

Years later, the Samantha Reed Mentorship Program continued to thrive, producing a steady stream of successful female entrepreneurs who themselves became mentors and role models. The Samantha Reed Foundation had expanded its reach, supporting countless women and girls across the nation. Samantha's name became synonymous with empowerment, resilience, and the unwavering belief in the potential of every woman to achieve greatness. Her influence was no longer confined to her own business; it had become deeply woven into the fabric of the Australian business community and beyond.

One could find echoes of Samantha's impact in the numerous female-led businesses that flourished, in the increased participation of women in leadership roles, and in the growing awareness of gender equality within corporate settings. Her legacy wasn't merely a historical record; it was a living, breathing entity that continued to inspire and empower generations of women to pursue their dreams and shape a better future. Samantha had achieved more than just building a successful business; she had built a lasting legacy, one that transcended her own achievements and extended its influence far into the future.

Her impact reached beyond the direct beneficiaries of her programs and initiatives. It inspired countless other individuals and organizations to create similar programs, to promote women's empowerment, and to advocate for gender equality in the workplace. Samantha's story sparked a wave of change, prompting discussions and reforms in policies and practices across numerous industries. The ripple effect of her contributions was far-reaching and profound.

She became a symbol of hope and possibility for countless women who had previously felt marginalized or excluded. Her story resonated with those who felt underestimated, overlooked, or simply doubted their own abilities. Samantha's journey provided tangible evidence that success wasn't about conforming to pre-defined expectations but about forging one's own path, pursuing one's passions, and having the unwavering courage to overcome obstacles.

The impact of her philanthropic work was particularly notable. The Samantha Reed Foundation didn't just provide financial assistance; it fostered a sense of community and belonging among its beneficiaries. It offered not only financial support but also crucial emotional support and guidance, creating a supportive network that empowered women to overcome challenges and achieve their full potential.

The media played a significant role in amplifying Samantha's message. Her story was featured in numerous prominent publications, documentaries, and television programs, bringing her message of empowerment to a vast audience. This widespread media coverage further cemented her status as a leading figure in the movement for women's empowerment.

Beyond the tangible achievements, Samantha's enduring influence lay in the shift in mindset she helped create. She fostered a culture of mentorship and collaboration, encouraging women to support and uplift one another. She created a space where women felt empowered to share their experiences, learn from one another, and celebrate each other's successes.

Her legacy is a reminder that true success is not solely defined by financial wealth or accolades. It's about making a meaningful impact on the lives of others, inspiring future generations, and leaving the world a better place than you found it. Samantha Reed embodied this philosophy, and her enduring influence serves as a beacon for aspiring female entrepreneurs and a testament to the enduring power of the human spirit. Her story continues to resonate, echoing through the halls of business and inspiring women everywhere to reach for their dreams, knowing that with hard work, determination, and unwavering belief in themselves, anything is possible.

CHAPTER 28
Inspiring a New Generation

The Samantha Reed Mentorship Program wasn't just another business initiative; it was a testament to Samantha's unwavering belief in the power of mentorship and the potential of women. She understood the unique challenges faced by women in the Australian business landscape – the subtle biases, the pervasive doubts, the uphill battles fought against ingrained societal expectations. She'd faced them all, and emerged victorious, not solely through sheer grit and talent, but through the invaluable support she'd received along the way. This understanding fueled her determination to create a program that offered comprehensive support, going beyond the typical business workshops and seminars.

The program wasn't limited to theoretical knowledge; it emphasized practical application and real-world experience. Participants weren't simply lectured; they were actively engaged in collaborative projects, case studies, and networking opportunities. Samantha believed that learning thrived in a supportive environment, a community where women could feel safe to share their vulnerabilities, celebrate their successes, and learn from each other's experiences. She carefully selected mentors – accomplished women from diverse industries, each possessing unique expertise and a genuine commitment to nurturing the next generation. These mentors weren't just advisors; they were confidantes, providing both professional guidance and emotional support.

One of the program's unique aspects was its focus on building resilience. Samantha knew that entrepreneurial journeys were rarely smooth; they were filled with setbacks, disappointments, and moments of self-doubt. Her program incorporated workshops on stress management, emotional intelligence, and overcoming adversity. She believed that equipping women with the tools to navigate the emotional rollercoaster of entrepreneurship was just as crucial as providing them with business acumen. The program also addressed the pervasive issue of imposter syndrome, a phenomenon disproportionately affecting women. Through group discussions, individual coaching, and success stories shared by mentors and alumni, the program helped participants challenge their self-limiting beliefs and embrace their accomplishments.

The impact of the program was profound and far-reaching. The women who participated were not just acquiring business skills; they were undergoing a transformation. They were learning to believe in their capabilities, to embrace their unique strengths, and to see their ambitions as attainable, not just wishful thinking. The program created a network of support that extended beyond the duration of the course, fostering a sense of community and camaraderie among participants. Many forged lifelong friendships and professional collaborations, bolstering each other through the challenges and triumphs of their entrepreneurial journeys. Success stories began to emerge, echoing Samantha's own journey.

Sarah, a young Indigenous Australian woman with a passion for sustainable fashion, used the program to launch her own ethical clothing line, employing local artisans and using ecofriendly materials. Her business, initially a small operation run from her garage, quickly expanded, becoming a successful brand that championed both sustainability and cultural preservation. Maria, a recent immigrant from Italy with a background in culinary arts, used the mentorship program to develop a unique catering business focusing on authentic Italian cuisine. Her dedication, combined with the business skills she acquired through the program, enabled her to establish a thriving business, gaining recognition for her culinary expertise and her contributions to the local community. And then there was Chloe, a single mother with a background in engineering who leveraged the program to start her own renewable energy company. Her innovative approach to solar energy solutions not only garnered her substantial investment but also made a tangible impact on the environment.

These stories weren't isolated incidents; they were indicative of a larger trend. The Samantha Reed Mentorship Program was empowering women from diverse backgrounds to become successful entrepreneurs, contributing to the Australian economy and inspiring future generations. The program's curriculum evolved over time, reflecting the changing landscape of the business world and incorporating feedback from participants. Samantha, even in her retirement, remained actively involved, offering guidance and support, attending networking events, and sharing her insights with the participants. Her presence wasn't just symbolic; it provided a constant reminder of the power of perseverance and the importance of giving back.

Beyond the tangible results, the program fostered a cultural shift. It challenged the traditional narrative that equated success solely with financial wealth or recognition. It redefined success to encompass social impact, personal growth, and the fulfillment that comes from contributing to something larger than oneself. This holistic approach resonated with the participants, many of whom were driven not just by profit motives but also by a desire to make a positive impact on their communities.

The program's success wasn't solely measured by financial metrics or the number of businesses launched. It was measured by the confidence exuded by its graduates, their willingness to take risks, and their determination to overcome obstacles. The program cultivated a sense of shared purpose and collective empowerment among women who, prior to participation, might have felt isolated and overwhelmed by the challenges of the business world. It created a powerful network of support, encouraging collaboration and mentorship among participants. Alumni often mentored new cohorts, passing on the knowledge and wisdom they had gained, perpetuating a cycle of giving back and fostering continuous growth.

Samantha's legacy extended far beyond her own entrepreneurial achievements. She had built an empire, but she also built a community, a legacy of empowerment that continued to thrive long after she stepped away from the day-to-day operations of her businesses. Her story, relayed through the successes of her mentees, became a powerful symbol of female empowerment in Australia and beyond. It became a story of resilience, perseverance, and the transformative power of mentorship and believing in oneself. It was a story that inspired countless women to pursue their entrepreneurial dreams, knowing that they didn't have to walk the path alone. Samantha's legacy wasn't merely a collection of business achievements; it was a living, breathing testament to the enduring power of the human spirit, a beacon illuminating the path for countless women to follow their own paths to success. And as the sun set on her remarkable life, the rising sun of a new generation of female entrepreneurs shone brighter than ever before, a testament to the lasting impact of Samantha Reed. Her story, in essence, had become the most powerful business lesson of all – the lesson of empowerment and unwavering belief in the face of adversity, a lesson that will continue to inspire for generations to come. The impact of her life extended far beyond her business empire, creating a ripple effect of empowerment that transcended borders and touched the lives of countless women. This is the true measure of a lasting legacy – one built not on personal gain but on the empowerment and success of others.

CHAPTER 29
A Symbol of Female Empowerment

The whispers of Samantha Reed's story, initially confined to the bustling boardrooms of Sydney, had begun to spread like wildfire. Her journey wasn't simply a rags-to-riches tale; it was a narrative of unwavering resilience, a testament to the strength of the human spirit, particularly the female spirit, in the face of seemingly insurmountable odds. It resonated deeply with women across Australia and beyond, striking a chord with those who'd faced similar battles—the subtle discrimination, the persistent doubts sown by societal expectations, the exhausting climb against a glass ceiling that often felt impenetrable.

Samantha hadn't just built a business empire; she'd built a movement. Her mentorship program, initially a small seed of an idea, had blossomed into a vibrant ecosystem, nurturing a new generation of female entrepreneurs. These weren't just women who had learned business strategies; they were women who had discovered a strength they never knew they possessed, women who now carried the torch of empowerment, passing it forward with the same unwavering belief that Samantha had instilled in them.

Aisha, one of Samantha's earliest mentees, started her business with a mere handful of handcrafted jewellery pieces sold from a stall at a local market. Today, her brand, "Desert Bloom," is internationally recognized, featuring in high-end boutiques and online marketplaces across the globe. Aisha credits Samantha not only for the business acumen she'd imparted but for the profound belief she fostered in Aisha's own capabilities. "Samantha taught me to see my limitations not as barriers but as opportunities for growth," Aisha recounts in countless interviews, her voice ringing with the conviction only a woman empowered can possess. "She showed me that fear was just a story I was telling myself, and that I had the power to rewrite it."

Then there was Zara, a young Indigenous woman from a remote community in Northern Australia. Samantha had personally championed Zara's participation in the mentorship program, recognizing the immense potential buried beneath systemic disadvantages. Zara, now the CEO of her own sustainable fashion label, showcasing the vibrant artistry of her people, spoke passionately about Samantha's mentorship. "She saw something in me that I didn't see in myself," Zara explains with a quiet strength. "She didn't just teach me business; she taught me self-belief, resilience, and the

importance of using my talents to uplift my community."

These weren't isolated instances; they were echoes of a broader transformation, a ripple effect emanating from Samantha's unwavering commitment to female empowerment. Her story had become a powerful symbol, a beacon illuminating the path for countless women who might have otherwise succumbed to doubt or despair. It was a story that transcended cultural boundaries, resonating with women in countries far removed from Australia's shores. Women who'd never met Samantha felt an inexplicable connection to her journey, recognizing the universality of the challenges she'd overcome.

News outlets across the globe featured Samantha's story. Documentaries were made, books were written, and conferences were held discussing her legacy and the transformative impact of the Samantha Reed Mentorship Program. The program itself became a case study in business schools, analyzing its unique approach to mentorship and its remarkable success in empowering women. The program's curriculum, which had evolved over the years, constantly adapted to the changing landscape of the business world, focusing on not just the technical skills needed for success, but also on building emotional resilience, fostering strong networks, and navigating the inherent challenges of gender bias.

The success stories of her mentees weren't just about financial achievements; they were about personal transformations, about women discovering their own strength, their own voices, and their own paths to success. It was about creating a sisterhood, a supportive network where women felt safe to share their vulnerabilities, celebrate their victories, and learn from each other's experiences. This sense of community was a key component of Samantha's legacy, a testament to her understanding that success is rarely achieved in isolation.

Samantha's impact extended beyond the business world. She became a vocal advocate for gender equality, using her platform to champion women's rights and challenge ingrained societal norms. She spoke at international conferences, addressed parliaments, and penned thoughtprovoking articles that sparked essential conversations on the importance of inclusivity, diversity, and fair representation in the workforce. Her work transcended the boundaries of business, inspiring social and political change.

Her influence permeated various aspects of society, influencing everything from corporate policies on maternity leave to the representation of women in media. Companies began to implement more inclusive hiring practices, acknowledging the value of diverse perspectives and the untapped potential of women. Educational institutions expanded their programs to foster female entrepreneurship, providing crucial resources and support to aspiring women in business.

Samantha's story resonated because it was authentic. It was a story of setbacks and triumphs, of moments of doubt and moments of unwavering determination. It was a story that celebrated vulnerability, not as a weakness, but as a source of strength. It was a testament to the power of perseverance, reminding women that the path to success is rarely a straight line. There would be obstacles, challenges, and moments of self-doubt, but through it all, the unwavering belief in oneself, the power of support and community, and the sheer tenacity of the human spirit are the driving forces of genuine, lasting change.

Moreover, Samantha's legacy wasn't just about her own achievements; it was about the ripple effect she created, the countless women she empowered to pursue their dreams, and the enduring change she inspired in the world. Her life became a living testament to the transformative power of mentorship, demonstrating that investing in others is not only a rewarding act but a powerful catalyst for societal progress.

Even years after her passing, Samantha's influence was palpable. Her mentorship program continued to flourish, expanding its reach and providing invaluable support to a growing number of female entrepreneurs worldwide. Her books were translated into numerous languages, spreading her message of empowerment and resilience across cultures and continents. Her story continues to be a source of inspiration, a reminder that anything is possible with hard work, determination, and the unwavering belief in oneself. The lasting legacy of Samantha Reed wasn't just about the business she built, it was about the community she fostered, the lives she touched, and the countless women she empowered to achieve their dreams. It was a legacy that would continue to inspire for generations to come, proving that true success is measured not only by personal achievements but also by the positive impact one makes on the world. Her story serves as a powerful reminder that each of us possesses the potential to create our own lasting legacy – a legacy of empowerment, inspiration, and unwavering belief in the potential of every woman to achieve their dreams and shape their own destinies. And that is, perhaps, the most valuable lesson of all. It is a legacy that continues to unfold, shaping the future, one empowered woman at a time.

CHAPTER 30
Reflecting on the Journey

The scent of eucalyptus hung heavy in the air, a familiar comfort as I sat on the veranda overlooking the sprawling Sydney Harbour. The sun dipped below the horizon, painting the sky in fiery hues of orange and purple, a fitting backdrop for reflecting on the extraordinary life of Samantha Reed. Her story, etched not just in the annals of Australian business but in the hearts of countless women worldwide, deserved a proper, contemplative ending. It wasn't just about the billions she amassed or the empire she built; it was about the unwavering spirit that fueled her journey.

Samantha's early life wasn't a fairy tale. It was a relentless struggle. Born into modest circumstances, she faced challenges most wouldn't even comprehend. The subtle yet pervasive sexism of the corporate world was a constant adversary, an invisible wall she had to repeatedly breach. There were moments of crippling self-doubt, times when the weight of expectation nearly crushed her. Yet, she persevered, fueled by an inner fire, an unyielding belief in her own potential that shone brighter than any obstacle. She learned to navigate the treacherous waters of the business world, not by conforming but by forging her own path. She was a pioneer, a trailblazer, carving out a space for herself and, in doing so, creating opportunities for generations of women to follow.

Remember the countless late nights spent poring over spreadsheets, the sacrifices she made, the times she pushed herself to the brink of exhaustion? These weren't just anecdotes; they were the bricks and mortar of her success. Each sleepless night, each moment of doubt overcome, sculpted her into the formidable businesswoman she became.

It wasn't a linear path, filled with easy victories. There were setbacks, failures, moments when even she questioned her ability to continue. Yet, from each stumble, she rose stronger, wiser, and more determined. This resilience, this ability to learn from adversity, was the bedrock of her extraordinary journey.

Her mentorship program, a testament to her belief in nurturing the next generation of female leaders, stands as a powerful symbol of her legacy. Countless women, initially hesitant and unsure, found in Samantha a beacon of hope, a mentor who understood their struggles, and a guide who helped them navigate the often-turbulent waters of entrepreneurship. The program wasn't merely about business strategies and financial planning; it was about fostering confidence, resilience, and the belief in one's own potential. It was about empowering women to become the architects of their own destinies.

The impact of her books, translated into countless languages, extends far beyond the commercial success they achieved. They became guides, companions, and sources of inspiration for women across cultures and continents. Her words resonated with those who had faced similar battles, those who had felt the sting of discrimination, the crushing weight of societal expectations. Samantha's story wasn't just hers; it became a universal narrative of resilience, empowerment, and the unwavering pursuit of dreams. It was a reminder that success isn't defined solely by material wealth but by the positive impact one has on the world.

Her philanthropic endeavors, often undertaken quietly and without fanfare, reflect a deep-seated compassion and a genuine desire to give back. She understood that true success was measured not only by personal achievement but also by the positive difference one makes in the lives of others. Her contributions to various women's charities and educational initiatives speak volumes about her commitment to social responsibility and her unwavering belief in the transformative power of education. These actions solidified her legacy, moving beyond mere financial success to a legacy of genuine and impactful philanthropy.

Thinking back, one can't help but be struck by the sheer magnitude of her accomplishments. The international business empire, the books that inspired millions, the mentorship program that continues to empower women across the globe – these were not the results of luck or chance, but the culmination of years of tireless work, unwavering determination, and an unshakeable belief in herself. It was the perfect blend of strategic planning, visionary leadership, and an exceptional understanding of the human spirit.

But her success wasn't solely a reflection of her business acumen; it was also a testament to her personal strength. She faced criticism, doubt, and adversity with grace, resilience, and an unwavering belief in her own abilities. She demonstrated that success was not a destination but a journey, a continuous process of learning, adapting, and growing. She showed the world that vulnerability wasn't weakness, but a source of strength, a catalyst for empathy and connection.

As the last rays of sunlight faded, leaving a soft twilight over the harbour, I felt a deep sense of gratitude for the opportunity to have known Samantha, even if only through the stories I had compiled. Her journey was a beacon, illuminating the path for women everywhere. She demonstrated that the glass ceiling, while formidable, is not unbreakable. With enough grit, determination, and an unwavering belief in oneself, anything is possible. Her legacy is not just about the financial success she achieved but about the countless lives she touched, the countless women she empowered, and the profound impact she had on the world.

The lasting impact of Samantha Reed extends far beyond the boardrooms and financial statements. It's in the quiet confidence of a young entrepreneur taking her first steps, the unwavering determination of a woman defying expectations, the supportive community of female leaders she inspired. It's in the ripple effect of empowerment, spreading across continents, changing lives, and shaping futures. Her story is a testament to the power of resilience, a powerful reminder that we all possess the strength to overcome adversity, to achieve our dreams, and to create a lasting legacy that inspires generations to come.

Samantha's story serves as a timeless reminder that true success is not solely measured by material possessions or financial achievements. It's about the impact we have on the lives of others, the positive changes we bring to the world, and the legacy of inspiration we leave behind. Her commitment to empowering women, her relentless pursuit of her goals, and her unwavering belief in her own abilities stand as a beacon of hope and a source of inspiration for all.

Her journey wasn't just about building a business; it was about building a community, a network of support, a legacy of empowerment. And this, perhaps, is the most enduring part of her story – the ripple effect of her influence, continuing to shape the lives of countless women, generation after generation. It's a legacy that transcends borders, languages, and cultures, a testament to the enduring power of the human spirit and the unwavering belief in oneself. Her legacy continues to inspire, to empower, to uplift – a silent testament to a woman who dared to dream big, and in doing so, changed the world. And that, my friends, is a truly lasting legacy. The sun finally set, leaving behind a starlit sky, a fitting end to a chapter that had inspired millions, a chapter of resilience, determination, and an unwavering belief in the power of the human spirit, particularly the indomitable spirit of women.

The story of Samantha Reed, a story etched in the hearts of millions, continues to inspire hope, resilience and the unwavering pursuit of dreams. It is a legacy that will continue to resonate for generations to come, proving that true success is not just about personal achievement, but about the positive impact we have on the world. It is a legacy that lives on, one empowered woman at a time.

Sandhiya Iyyappan is a female author and entrepreneur with a passion for inspiring women to pursue their dreams. She is the author of the compelling love story "Against All Odd" by Sandhiya Iyyappan. Having built her own successful business, she combines creative storytelling with real-world business acumen in her writing. Her work focuses on empowering narratives that celebrate female ambition, resilience, and the pursuit of success. Beyond writing inspirational fiction, she also contributes regularly to various platforms, sharing insights on entrepreneurship and personal growth. *Her Kingdom, Her Creation* embodies her belief that every woman has the power to achieve greatness, and her stories aim to ignite that spark within readers.